THE MAESTRO

ITALIAN ROMANCE STORIES
VOLUME 3

MADDI MAGRÌ

The Maestro
Copyright 2023 Maddi Magrì
All rights reserved.
Translated from Italian by R. Ricci
Original title: Il violoncellista
Copyright 2021 Maddi Magrì
All rights reserved.

This book is a work of fiction. Every reference to real people, places and events is reworked from the imagination. The other names, characters, places and events are products of the creativity of the author and any resemblance to real events, places or people, living or dead, is purely coincidental.

CHAPTER 1.

Pantone green number number 376. Virginia had miraculously sourced ties that matched the color of the napkins to a tee. She'd had them speedily dispatched to the football team members, for whom she was hosting a reception that was nothing short of a jamboree.

The soirée was a dual celebration, marking the centenary of the club's birth—a quirky twist of fate that also aligned with the CEO's son's birthday. Virginia's plan was to color the entire party in acid green and daffodil yellow, the team's colors. She'd scoured the Earth (okay, not the entire planet, maybe just Milan) for accessories that seamlessly blended these two lively hues. Picture this: yellow tablecloths that practically sang next to the fresh green napkins.

But those ties? Oh, they were the pièce de résistance. Well, until that fateful moment near the end of the night when a man, his back to one of the tables, casually flung his tie onto a stack of similarly hued napkins—probably to protect it from a stray spaghetti sauce assault. At that moment, a young boy had come running and without realizing it, had quickly grabbed the napkin on top, which was none other than the poor gentleman's tie. The poor soul, in a desperate bid to avoid asphyxiation, tumbled in a rather ungraceful manner.

Virginia immediately rushed over, at first not understanding what had happened and only later, realizing that the child could not have actually noticed the difference between the napkin and the tie, began to apologize profusely.

In an otherwise pitch-perfect evening, this hiccup was entirely hers. She, the guardian of seamless execution, had screwed up.

Virginia continued to mull over the episode that would surely cost her the advancement in rank she was hoping for, as she climbed into the cab, heading for Malpensa Airport.

Mr. Siveri, the founder of SiVery Event—a boutique agency that orchestrated jaw-dropping events for corporate and private clients—was insistent on one thing: flawless execution, no excuses, with everyone in their designated place, each task well-defined, and coordination that could rival a ballet performance. Virginia was one of the four top managers entrusted by Siveri to tend to the clients' every need. As the taxi driver handed over her suitcase and she handed him the fare, Virginia let out a heavy sigh, knowing that her journey might just be the prelude to a rather unwelcome outcome—maybe even the end of the road for her cherished position.

The office had been buzzing about this meeting for months, and everyone was gearing up for a two-day training and team-building extravaganza. It was an outbound trip from Milan to Vienna on December 21st, with the return leg on December 23rd, just before the Christmas Holidays. At home, in her suitcase, she'd packed a couple of suits and a range of casual outfits. But for the journey, she had chosen to wear her best outfit: a chic black jacket nipped at the waist, matching a knee-length, high-waisted skirt. The outfit had a magnetic quality, thanks to a row of delicate, shiny buttons that accentuated her curves. She'd initially planned to go for an elegant and alluring look because there was a welcome party slated for that evening, followed by a gala dinner. She scrutinized the silk cream-colored shirt she'd selected. It had a unique collar that fastened like a tie, with just a couple of buttons—one at heart level and another at the waist to cinch it all together. Completing the ensemble were sleek black patent leather shoes with a towering twelve-inch heel, ensuring she'd make a commanding entrance. This outfit had been meticulously planned long before the unfortunate green napkin incident, and now, with no time for a plan B, frustration gnawed at her. The trip to Vienna was definitely not going to pan out as she'd envisioned.

Every year, during these gatherings, her boss would single out a few colleagues for praise and, in his typically unsubtle style, unveil a coveted promotion. Until recently, she had been convinced that she would be the one to take center stage this year. Instead, it seemed that someone else would be taking the limelight.

She stepped into the airport, where her colleagues had already congregated, forming a huddle reminiscent of a flock of sheep at the gate.

"Oh, gosh!" she thought, eyes wide as she surveyed the bustling crowd. "Wasn't it supposed to be just us going to Vienna?!" She couldn't believe the number of people cramming into the seats, all while the anticipation of a seemingly endless wait before boarding a plane for a mere hour-and-a-half flight weighed on her.

Then, there was Martina, her ever-observant colleague. "Virginia, over here! We saved you a seat. It's a bit of a delay, though. They've canceled some flights," she informed her with a sympathetic smile.

Dragging her trolley with a hint of resignation, Virginia made her way toward the small group—her team: Martina, Claudio, and Elisabetta. She had no illusions; she knew they were deep into their happy gossip session, just waiting to unfold the latest chapter of office indiscretions. And she didn't begrudge them that pleasure one bit.

Elisabetta piped up half-heartedly, "Have you seen Gloria's outfit?"

"Oh God, I was telling Gianni just last night. I'm sorry but that girl simply does not know how to dress," Claudio chimed in. Virginia had always liked Claudio; he exuded culture and refinement, and when she discovered his meticulous tendencies, she had naturally taken him under her wing. They worked together with an easy rapport, and she felt she could trust him implicitly. It was a stark contrast to Martina, who, while generally good-natured, could be a touch too acerbic at times. Thankfully, Claudio knew how to keep Martina's sharpness at arm's length.

Then there was Elisabetta, petite and pretty, always worried with her little son, firmly believing that the entire world revolved around him. Elia's eating, Elia's talking, Elia's playing... They had a detailed knowledge of every bathroom visit little Elia made, just in case they ever had a burning curiosity. But beyond that, she was a diligent worker, and as far as Virginia was concerned, that was the only thing that truly mattered.

Elisabetta's comment broke through Virginia's thoughts, pulling her back into their conversation. "She keeps dressing like that because she's hoping Cantarini will notice her. Can't you see how she's sticking to him? She'd love to be on his team. It seems that Siveri has a soft spot for him, and I think she might call him up on stage tonight..." Elisabetta's words hung in the air, drawing Virginia's incredulous response.

"A soft spot? For Luigi?" Virginia asked, her disbelief evident.

They all turned toward her in unison, their expressions conveying that she had just asked the most obvious of questions. Martina, in her characteristically sarcastic tone, chimed in, "Virginia, where have you been living? Don't you know it's almost a sure thing he's getting that promotion? It's practically in the air. Someone heard from Carolina that Siveri's planning to reshuffle the entire organizational chart just for him..."

"Well, that's just great," Virginia replied wryly, her mind mulling over her own position within the company. She wanted to put an end to the chatter, so she added, "Wake me up when they start boarding." She lowered a sleep mask over her eyes, inserted earplugs, and crossed her arms, attempting to get some rest.

Half an hour later, Claudio gently touched her arm. "Wake up, we're boarding!"

A throng of passengers had congregated at the exit, and Virginia sighed in frustration. She had no intention of queuing up like everyone else. "I'll catch up with you. Go ahead."

Waiting until the last person had entered the

plane, Virginia finally rose from her seat. She smoothed her blouse and skirt, then made her way toward the flight attendants with a friendly smile.

"Good morning," she greeted one of them. "Here's my passport..."

But her words trailed off as the stewardess became distracted, her attention drawn elsewhere. Virginia turned to see what had captured her gaze. A group of five men, all dressed in sleek black attire, was marching toward the gate with military precision. The leader, towering in height and oozing confidence, strolled confidently with an air of authority. He carried nothing in his hands, in stark contrast to the others who lugged trolleys and bulky musical instrument cases.

The other flight attendants had converged around the men, or rather, around the one man with a capital "M," the undeniable leader, the alpha male who had also captured Virginia's attention.

"Oh, what a fine specimen he is," Virginia mused silently. "I suppose I'm a tad short for him, even with my heels..."

As the group filed past the entrance to the gate, Virginia turned her attention back to the flight attendant. "Where were we?" she prompted, waving her passport to resume their conversation.

"Ah, yes, thank you," the flight attendant responded. "Today is your lucky day, we've had overbooking in Economy, so we need to upgrade you to Business. I'll inform my colleague. Please bring your suitcase with you; there's plenty of room in Business.."

"Oh, how nice, thank you!" Virginia's words were met with a tone that hinted at inconvenience, but she couldn't have been happier. As she made her way into the cabin, she couldn't resist turning to Claudio and Martina, who were seated in Economy.

"So sorry dears!" she announced with a smile, pointing dramatically toward the front of the plane.

"Nooo, you lucky girl!" Claudio exclaimed, and she waved back at him.

The curtain dividing the two sections led her to believe she was moving from a cramped, noisy space to a more spacious one. To her surprise, the business class was quite small, and it was already occupied by the five men she'd seen earlier at the gate. They were seated on both sides, close to the windows, with their bags and cases occupying the seats nearby.

The only available spot for her was in the aisle near the curtain dividing the business from the economy section, as the window-side seats were taken. The right to enjoy the window seat had been reserved for a colossal musical instrument case belonging to one of the men from the group.

What could it be? And, above all, does a

musical instrument have the right to stay in business? And in a window seat?

Virginia sighed in frustration. The flight attendants appeared to be occupied elsewhere, so she took it upon herself to stow her coat and trolley in the overhead compartment. She then settled into her seat and fastened her seatbelt.

"Just my luck..." she muttered under her breath.

Spotting a flight attendant in the distance, Virginia raised her arm to signal for assistance. She planned to ask them to move the bulky case blocking her view. However, her attempts went unnoticed. Another flight attendant emerged, but it seemed they were all tending to the energetic man seated in the front row, whose distinctive forelock she could glimpse.

She shifted uncomfortably and caught a sidelong glance from one of the flight attendants. The attendant approached her swiftly and spoke curtly, "We're about to take off, and as we mentioned earlier, we need to rearrange things. We'll bring your welcome drink after take off." The tone was categorical, bordering on impolite. Virginia didn't even have a chance to respond before the flight attendant returned to the man's side.

I didn't even request a drink! Ah whatever!

She slumped into her seat, tilting her head

back and closed her eyes, catching some rest during the stewardess's safety instructions, the captain's greetings, and takeoff procedures. When the aircraft reached its cruising altitude, she decided it was time for a bathroom break, preparing herself for the welcome flute of champagne.

The restroom was free, as indicated by the green light. The path to the restrooms though, seemed to be blocked. Blocked, that is, by the striking alpha male musician. She briefly glanced back at the curtain dividing the sections of the plane and then returned her gaze forward. She had no intention of navigating through the tumultuous sea of economy class passengers, let alone engaging in casual chatter with her colleagues about mundane matters.

She got up and made her way toward the restroom. Alpha man was entirely blocking the entrance, engrossed in his cell phone, leaning against the doorframe, with his left foot propped halfway in, and the other on the floor. His slightly wavy blond hair cascaded, obscuring his face from Virginia's view. He was dressed in a snug black polo shirt and would occasionally scratch his chin. Virginia adjusted her glasses and hesitated.

"Excuse me," she managed to utter, her voice barely above a whisper.

The man simply raised his face toward her and nonchalantly said, "Go ahead, if you need to use the restroom..." but he didn't budge an inch.

"What a nice guy," Virginia thought sarcastically. She wasn't quite sure how to maneuver this situation. Despite her heels bordering on the vertiginous, the behemoth blocking her path was significantly taller than her, making the prospect of getting past him seem daunting.

All right, if you think you can stop me, you're dead wrong! she thought, mustering up the determination to make her way to the restroom. With a touch of defiance, she leaned on the man's arm to clamber over him.

Their eyes locked, and he sported a mocking grin that was perfectly complemented by his sharply defined jawline, tanned oval face, and a nose that could be described as nothing less than perfect—classically Roman. But it was his gaze that truly held her attention. The man possessed the greenest eyes Virginia had ever encountered. Without even realizing it, she found her eyes slowly tracing up and down his biceps, studying the contours of his well-sculpted muscles. Was his turtleneck a size too small, or were those muscles just exceptionally pronounced?

Oh God, listen to me talking nonsense!

She was flustered, her gaze locked onto his chest and arms, a sudden rush of adrenaline and agitation surging through her, causing her to wobble.

Or perhaps it was just an air pocket jostling the plane?

"Are you all right?" the man asked, gently steadying her by the arm. She managed to move her leg, albeit somewhat shakily.

Just then, a flight attendant arrived, extending a flute to the man who greeted her with a cheerful, "Oh, just what I needed. Thank you!"

Even his voice is sexy! Virginia thought, her head spinning. She found herself irked by the high-pitched tone of the stewardess as she obligingly replied, "You're welcome, Maestro," before turning with a flirtatious chuckle and sashaying back toward the galley.

"She's as flustered as I am, just to be near this walking embodiment of testosterone. Then again, who can blame her?" Virginia mused.

Suddenly, the pieces of the puzzle clicked into place for Virginia, and she had a moment of clarity about biology and her high school teacher, Professor Bandini.

The 'Maestro' flashed a sly smile and gestured toward the service door. "I was saying, go ahead. I'm not in line."

Uhm, is he Pantone green number 348 or number 349? Virginia wondered, captivated by the man's eyes that never seemed to look down.

Swallowing hard, she finally closed the bathroom door and leaned against the frame. She held her head high, pondering the inexplicable attraction she felt for a man she had barely spoken to. Her breathing grew labored as she rinsed her hands and splashed her face.

"Pull yourself together!" she scolded herself inwardly, determined to regain her composure.

Virginia's heart raced as she reapplied her makeup, her raspberry lipstick gliding over her full, heart-shaped lips, which she considered her best feature. Like a schoolgirl with a crush, she began to assess her chances of catching his eye. She made a few adjustments to her bra, aware of her modest C cup.

Tightening the knot of her ponytail, she wondered if perhaps she should have let her hair down, allowing it to cascade more freely, especially for someone like him. But her long black hair was always pulled back meticulously, a picture of perfection, even on this particular day. Then again, she was on a business trip, she reminded herself, sighing in mild frustration.

A touch of mascara on her eyebrows to add depth, but aside from the lipstick, she preferred to leave her soft, rosy skin untouched by cosmetics. Although now, she couldn't help but think that a little more makeup might have enhanced her features, maybe made her nose appear less, well, potato-like, as her father affectionately called it.

"But what will he think?" she fretted, her anxiety mounting. "Oh, dear..."

She sighed once more, scolding herself for feeling like a giddy schoolgirl. It's not as if he's out there waiting just for me, she reasoned.

With a deep breath, she opened the bathroom door, her gaze initially falling to the shiny black shoes outside. Ferragamo, surely, she thought. She gradually lifted her eyes to find him. This time, the man was facing her, toward the bathroom door. Was he really waiting for her?

"All done?" he inquired with an amused smile.

Virginia felt her cheeks flush, but she managed to nod. Her lips tingled, and she ran her tongue slowly over them. The man smiled, tracing his mouth with the thumb of the hand holding a glass.

"Care for some champagne?" he offered, not waiting for a response as he lightly took Virginia's arm and guided her toward nearby seats. "Come, let's have a seat."

He turned to the flight attendant. "Stefania, one more, please!" Then he gestured for Virginia to slide into the window seat. "Go ahead," he urged, following her and settling beside her. His left leg lightly brushed against hers, and she attempted to discreetly inch away, but to no avail.

The flight attendant rushed over, a bright smile on her face as she chirped, "Yes, Maestro

Nucci?"

"Could you bring another one of these, for the young lady..." He turned to Virginia, raising his champagne flute as he introduced himself. "Guglielmo Nucci." He exuded an air of sharp decisiveness.

"Pleasure to meet you. Virginia Ranieri," she replied, slightly flustered.

The flight attendant arrived with a cart loaded with small bottles and an extra glass, which she handed to Virginia with a less-than-friendly look. She then proceeded to open the small table and bent down to arrange the tray for Guglielmo.

Is it me, or does she have her shirt partially unbuttoned at the chest? Really? Is she flirting with him too?

Virginia couldn't help but wonder, her thoughts slipping out a bit too candidly.

That "too" had slipped out unintentionally, making her feel awkward, so she shifted slightly in her seat. Guglielmo glanced at her curiously but was soon distracted by the excited flight attendant who asked, "Maestro Nucci, can we take a selfie together?"

"With pleasure," he agreed, leaning in for the photo.

Their arms were practically touching, faces too close for comfort in Virginia's opinion, and she watched as they posed, smiled, and clicked.

"Thank you, Maestro! Thank you!" The flight attendant acted as if he were a god, which, in a way, he was, but Virginia remained perplexed.

Who the heck is this guy? She wondered, her gaze fixed on him, as she tried to recall TV shows, social media feeds, magazine features, but nothing clicked.

"You too?" Guglielmo asked her.

"Excuse me?"

"Would you like a selfie with me as well?"

"Me? No, of course not!" she responded, laughing as if he'd made a clever joke. She could tell from his expression and the way he hastily consumed his champagne that he was hurt. So, she attempted to make amends. "I mean, I don't want to trouble you."

"No trouble at all. Please..." he said, regaining his smile as he leaned toward her. Virginia felt the warmth of his body and the touch of his hand on her knee. She cleared her throat and retrieved her cell phone from her breast pocket.

At least I can text Sara later; she's always up to date on every new influencer. She'll tell me who this man is, she thought. She opened her camera in selfie mode, posed, smiled, and took the photo. Guglielmo tilted his face toward her once more, and she barely turned her head.

God, he's handsome, she couldn't help but

think as she slipped her phone back into her pocket and mumbled a shy thank you. Her hormones were already plotting ways to get closer to him again.

"I'm used to it by now," Guglielmo said casually, as if assuming she knew who he was. "Back in the days, I was surprised and overwhelmed, but it only lasted a few weeks. You get used to fame quickly." He chuckled and adjusted his pants, perching on the edge of his seat, one arm resting on the headrest, turned toward Virginia. "I'm always delighted to make a fan happy. Have you ever been to one of my concerts?"

Virginia's gaze remained fixed on his biceps, and a brief silence hung between them.

Guglielmo lowered his head, shaking it. "You really don't know who I am, do you?" Now he sounded somewhat resentful.

Virginia fiddled with her shirt's buttons, wondering what to say. What do I tell him? She pondered, feeling a bit lost.

The man clicked his tongue, amazed. He took one end of the fake tie and slipped it between his fingers.

"I must say I'm surprised. I'm a cellist and world-renowned, too. I've even played in the White House! And you... you don't know me? You're the first woman I've met who doesn't know anything about me at all."

Oh, poor thing, I must have offended you!

"Um, Maestro," she said, trying to maintain some distance, "I'm afraid I don't follow the classical music scene much, I'm sorry. And before, I didn't mean to..."

Silence. The man stared at her, with a rather equivocal smile.

"Are you telling me you took the picture, just to please me?"

"Well you seemed to care so much for it..."

"Ha, ha, ha..." he laughed, throwing back his head and the row of white teeth lit up his face. "*I* seemed to care! That's a good one!"

Virginia stood up. "Well, I won't bother you any further, I'm going back to my seat." She told him decisively.

You may be good-looking, but you're also an arrogant a##!

Slipping past the coffee table and the man's body, Virginia felt a momentary sensation as if the Maestro's muscles, every single one of them, were pressing against her. She shot him a glance brimming with animosity, meeting his malicious stare head-on.

Returning to her seat, Virginia fastened her seatbelt and gazed out of the window. She took another sip of her champagne, trying to remain composed. While the sky outside was clear, her internal landscape felt turbulent, and she eagerly awaited the landing. As soon as the wheels screeched upon touchdown, she grabbed her trolley and coat, impatient to leave.

"Virgi! How did it go? Were you showered with admiration and reverence?" Claudio inquired eagerly from a few seats away as soon as he spotted her.

She nodded in response but remained aloof, maintaining her distance until they reached the hotel where they would be staying.

CHAPTER 2.

The hotel where they were staying was a five-star, located in the center of Vienna, a few minutes' walk from the imperial palace. Virginia looked at the quaint shop windows adorned with Christmas displays.

Another Christmas alone, she thought.

Perhaps love just isn't in the cards for me.

As the taxi passed in front of the Staatsoper opera house, Claudio told them the poignant love story of the two architects, Eduard van der Nüll and August Sicard von Sicardsburg, who had designed the edifice together. Virginia barely caught snippets of the tale.

"... did not attend the opening night... The two," Claudio explained, "had begun work before the Ringstrasse was raised about three feet above the road surface... the theater appeared as if it had sunk into the ground... it was nicknamed the sunken casket... and the architects were criticized to the point that Eduard committed suicide."

"Oh no!" exclaimed Elisabetta, bringing a hand to her mouth. Virginia turned sharply, back with them.

"Oh yes dear, he was only 56 years old... And that's not all, after only two months August also died, they say of a broken heart. And he was 55, like me."

"Uh," Elisabetta fanned her face to stop the tears. "Oh, it's heartbreaking. When I think about me and Valerio.... Do you know that when we were young, my parents didn't want us to get married at all?"

Elisabetta was made that way. She had a knack for linking every story to her own life or to her son Elia's. Virginia, at that moment, couldn't bear to listen to her musings again. She had only one thing on her mind: the Maestro. She let out a sigh of relief when the cab stopped in front of the hotel. "I'll take care of this, you guys go on inside and do your check in. I have to make a couple of calls, I'll be out here for a while."

In fact, she couldn't take it anymore from the other two. They weren't to blame, but her encounter with Guglielmo Nucci had consumed her entirely. She had to figure out who on earth he was, so she sent a photo to Sara, hoping for some answers.

Only two minutes ticked by, and her friend was already jabbering on the phone without a proper hello. "Oh my God! Tell me I'm dreaming!"

"So, you know who he is?"

"What do you mean, Virgi?"

"I mean, I've got no clue who this guy is. All I know is that my hormones have gone bonkers, and I'm still trying to rein them in!"

"Jeez, Virgi, what planet are you on?" exclaimed Sara.

"Evidently, on Mars! Today's the second time someone's said that to me! I, unlike the rest of you, work! And I mind my own business!" she ranted. "Sorry, Sara, I'm not mad at you. Maybe I work too much and miss out on a lot of things..."

"No worries, honey. And it's true, you work too much! And I guess you're still flustered. I get it, I'd be too, because the guy you met is none other than Guglielmo Nucci, the cellist! You seriously don't know who he is?! He played at the White House too!"

"Yes, I know, he told me..."

"Oh my gosh...you even talked to him?!"

"Yeah, a bit. I told him I didn't know him, and I think he got upset."

"No, come on, you said that?! Are you nuts! Every time there's a post about him, it takes me like a day to see Massimo normally again... I mean, let's face it, I love Massimo, but the Maestro rocks my world. Why did this happen to you and not to me?!"

Sara was firing questions. "This is so cool! What's he like in person? Are his muscles really like in the pictures? And that smile, I could watch his videos all day! Have you seen him perform live?"

Okay, so clearly, Sara's hormones are totally fixated on him too, Virginia thought. It's as if he's the last man on Earth.

She glanced up and caught a colleague, Paolo Corri, passing by, offering a nod in greeting. She reciprocated courteously.

Yes, definitely Guglielmo is the last male specimen left on earth. And what a specimen.

She nodded to herself, trying to make sense of it all, then resumed her conversation with her friend.

"No, I haven't seen him play...Sara, that's cool though. I'm still bewildered! Even if he is a little, how shall I put it... arrogant."

"Who cares! So," Sara continued, "let me enlighten you: he's part of the Four Bows, they tour globally and have been in the spotlight for ages. His private life's a mystery. Except for two things: he donates all his earnings to charity, and he's always surrounded by beautiful women. His last girlfriend was his agent, a former Brazilian lingerie model. Anyway, they split last year, and now he seems unattached. Oh, you're making me so envious! Can I share the photo with Monica? Please... Oh, and I've already tweaked it, added my face to it, and set it as my screensaver. After your rant, you owe me."

"Everything to charity? What, he lives of air?"

"Oh, well, I think he's made enough money that he can do as he pleases."

"Mmm generous with everyone, I mean, not just women... Listen, I have to go now. I still have to check in... I'll call you later. And go ahead and send Monica the picture too, at least she'll feast her eyes..."

The hotel lobby sprawled wide, and her colleagues were still in queue at the check-in desk. She slumped onto one of the couches and promptly googled 'Guglielmo Nucci'.

A slew of sites appeared reporting info about him and the quartet he was a part of.

She chose 'images' on Google. Basically it was a photoshoot dedicated to Guglielmo, while the other three members of the Four Bows appeared on the sidelines, in a few photos, as page boys.

Music awards, London, New York, Paris, the Maestro playing, the Maestro with a woman (clearly a model), the Maestro with many women (clearly all models).

Teatro alla Scala, Milan, Guglielmo with a blonde, her breasts literally resting on his arm.

The Maestro with three women, all in ecstasy.

The three graces.

She laughed. And she sighed, thinking about how many women the man had at his feet. How could she blame him, he didn't even have to make the effort to look for them. All vying for him, no questions asked.

Virginia made the comparison to her own list

as she contemplated her name. *Nomen omen*, the name is a sign, as the latins said in Ancient Rome. Including Carletto, her stories could be counted on the fingers of one hand. The first, at eight years old, had been Carletto, who, however, used to pick his nose before asking her to shake his hand. In no uncertain terms, she had told him that he could never become her boyfriend that way. At fifteen, however, it had been Raffaello's turn. The problem was that he never looked her in the face. As soon as they met, all he did was respond in monosyllables and, with his head down, staring at her chest. She gave him a resounding slap in the face when, after only four dates, he allowed himself to touch her. There had been the turn of Filippo, a close friend, but although they thought they were attracted to each other, when they had had their first kiss, they had stared at each other knowing that the famous alchemy hadn't even remotely clicked. A shame, because she was fine with him. Alessandro came along at nineteen, her first real boyfriend. Their first intimate encounter in a car was awkward, the subsequent times less so, but nothing remarkable. Finally, Luca, at the time she was attending university, who she thought was the one because of his tenderness when they made love. He turned out to be right for Carlotta instead, as she found out one night at her dorm.

The notifications on her phone chat had gone

crazy. She opened the chat and read the messages Monica and Sara had exchanged, as soon as Sara had sent the picture of her and Guglielmo. She had the chance to observe better how she had come: she could clearly see that she was agitated, next to the Maestro. She understood the reaction of other women. That man was dangerous.

Virginia was tired and just wanted to go to her room, so she closed the tabs and chat and walked over to the concierge to check in. There didn't seem to be anyone there. Actually, no, there were two girls, but they were both at the VIP desk. They were handling Guglielmo Nucci's check in.

"Mr. Nucci, your room is 501. You have a VIP upgrade with Champagne, full access to the spa, and complimentary full board. Hope it meets your satisfaction. Shall we take your luggage upstairs?"

Guglielmo glanced at Virginia, nodding to her with a smirk. "Yes, thank you. My instrument too, please," he added, putting emphasis on the word 'instrument.'

Virginia, irritated, dropped her bag on the counter. "Excuse me, can one of you two check me in as well?"

"One moment, ma'am. Please be patient," one of the girls responded.

"Patient, my foot," Virginia muttered, tapping on the counter in frustration.

The cellist chuckled. "Ah, assertive. I like that."

Virginia, without thinking, quipped back, "You haven't seen anything yet."

Guglielmo played along, widening his arms dramatically, the coat revealing his athletic build. "Careful now, tiger, I could take you on!"

Inside, Virginia mused how much she'd love that challenge. But she kept quiet, giving him a playful wink. The hotel staff, caught in the middle, finally handed her the room key, unsure of how to respond to their exchange.

By the time Virginia reached the elevators, Guglielmo and his crew had already departed. She entered her room, contemplating her bold interaction with the Maestro. Fatigue had stripped away her inhibitions; secretly, she wished for a different evening with him. Instead, she was among her colleagues, anticipating someone else winning the coveted company prize. Disheartened, she noticed it was already eight o'clock. It was late, she had to make her way down.

Virginia descended to the meeting room reserved for the SiVery dinner. The tables were elegantly set, seemingly dancing in front of the stage adorned with the company's logo. She wasn't slated to present anything, and given her current state, she didn't mind.

Virginia joined her colleagues, quietly sipping her wine while they chattered away. Mister Siveri's arrival marked a shift, but her engagement remained strictly with the wineglass. After three-quarters of an hour, Siveri entered, bypassing any preamble and launching into his welcome speech.

"Dear all. How lovely to see you here," Siveri began, his pauses deliberate. "For many of you, this may be the first glimpse of my face. Don't worry, you haven't missed much. But I, on the other hand, know each and every one of you. It may sound like a threat, but it is not. Anyone who has worked here for any length of time knows that teamwork is important to me. In a company like ours, details are key..."

Virginia struggled to focus. It was the same spiel—collaboration, teamwork, success, repeat.

Siveri concluded his speech with applause and a "Thank you all!" The room erupted in smiles and applause, but Virginia wasn't buying it. She loathed these theatrics and wished the evening would end there. Her only anticipation was to hear the name of the employee chosen to ascend the stage with the boss—a moment that arrived swiftly.

"Well, well. In that spirit, tonight I want to showcase someone who's been invaluable to us. Luigi Cantarini, come join me on stage."

Siveri presented a small trophy to Luigi. His name was expected, but hearing it from Siveri triggered a pang in Virginia's stomach. She feigned a cough to cover her reaction, seething inwardly.

"Thank you," Siveri commended Luigi, praising his contributions. Dinner followed, waiters served courses, and the atmosphere turned convivial. Virginia, attempting to distract herself, smiled but found no enjoyment. She was livid. She should have been on that stage, deserving recognition for nights spent coordinating every event detail.

Damn SiVery Event.

Damn ties and damn acidic green—the color as sour as her stomach in that moment.

Virginia glanced at her watch—it was nearly ten-thirty. She hoisted her Chanel pochette over her shoulder.

You know what? I deserve a trophy, too! She thought.

With a mischievous expression she said to her colleagues, "I'm going to bed..."

"Come on, Virginia, stay a bit more. Later, we'll dance!" said Martina to her, trying to talk her out of it.

I shall dance now, my dear, she thought, but took on a composed expression as she apologized, "Ah, no, no, thank you. I'd rather rest and be ready for tomorrow's trials..."

More smiles and farewells and finally off to the elevators. They were very small, decorated with wood and wrought iron inserts, in keeping with the hotel's Art Nouveau style. Fifth floor. "Phew," she huffed. Maybe she was fooling around, but she still had that trembling feeling on her, those muscles calling out to her. She needed to be urged on.

She opened the phone chat with her friends and typed: I know what the Maestro's room number is, what should I do?

Within moments, she hadn't even hit send yet, that the two friends had already gone wild with misspelled and hurried messages, correctly retyped but written in all caps, GIFs that said in bright, bold letters: GO! What are you waiting for?!!!???? Go!

She laughed and slipped her phone into her jacket pocket and felt it vibrating for notifications.

I'm going, I'm going...

Room 501, halfway down the hall. Further along, to the left side, was 502.

She lowered her head. "Oh God, what am I doing?" she muttered, as her fisted hand lightly touched the door. Two taps.

She let out an excited giggle as the door opened. She heard a male voice say, "Well, that was quick!"

Virginia's smiling expression turned into a totally inebriated one. Guglielmo occupied the entire doorway with his bare chest and biceps and above all, he had a towel at belly level, but not as taut as one would have expected, but rather saggy, as if he had put it there in front, just to be fair, not because he didn't want to be seen.

"Oh, it's you!" he exclaimed, surprised.

"Oh, it's you!" she replied, looking down clearly.

They both laughed, but she couldn't resist her own witticism and blushed. She felt her cheeks heat up and began to babble.

"I'm sorry, I..." the voice came out as if flooded. "I didn't want to bother you."

"No, no, bother at all," he told her and stepped forward, resting the arm with which he held the towel, on the doorframe. The piece came down a little.

Virginia tried not to move, but felt embarrassed to be so close to him.

"Well, I was wondering if-"

A voice, from inside the room, meowed, "Who is it?"

It was a woman's voice.

Uh, is this seat taken? Prizes tonight are being taken by others, what a drag... Loser across the board....

She stared at the emerald green eyes in front of her, which had become more intense. Because they were so close, she was able to determine, beyond a reasonable doubt, that those eyes were Pantone green number 348.

And that she was prospect number 25,000.

She spun on her heels and made to leave, but his hand grabbed her wrist firmly.

"Hey, where are you going, Virginia?"

Oh, well, at least he remembers my name. With all the women he has at his feet, that wasn't a given.

Facing him, she swayed a little, projecting confidence. "I'm heading to my room. To sleep. Forgive me if I interrupted a private moment." Internally, she blinked at the situation's abrupt turn.

He seemed indifferent to her words, pressing on, "Come on, Virginia, tell me why you came..." With a swift movement, he shut the door and adjusted his towel, still gripping her hand.

She tried to pull away, "It doesn't matter, really."

He released her momentarily, adjusting the unruly towel before taking a decisive step forward. "We're here now." His arms crossed, indicating he expected an explanation.

"All right..." She mirrored his stance, folding her arms in defiance. "I work for an event planning company, SiVery Event. I thought your quartet might be interested in high-end events." Retrieving her business card from her purse, she extended it toward him. "Here, I wanted to leave this with you."

Taking the card without a glance, he

approached her, backing her against the wall.

"Virginia, Virginia, Virginia..." He leaned his arms against the wall, encircling her, and brought his mouth close to hers. "You've never heard me play and yet you want to count me among your roster of musicians?"

Virginia remained impassive. She stood on her tiptoes, rubbing her chest against his, and with a whisper, replied, "And, on the other hand, you, you haven't even asked me out and you think you can count me already among your conquests?"

The cellist laughed slyly.

In a flash, with both hands, Virginia grabbed the biceps of his right arm, ducked, and broke free of the siege. Her voice came out determined.

"Think about it, Maestro. You have my number!" With a dismissive gesture, she headed straight for the elevator. She clicked the button, looked up to see the floor numbers light up, slowly, until the doors opened. She stepped inside and, without turning around, pressed the button for her floor. Her heartbeat was pounding and only when she sensed the doors closing behind her did she turn around.

Guglielmo stood in the middle of the hallway watching her, exuding undeniable virility.

MADDI MAGRÌ

CHAPTER 3.

The next day, Virginia strutted in, sporting her black thermal romper with fuchsia highlights, a smug smile playing on her lips. She was geared up for the Mud Run race—a daring move considering Vienna's unsuitability for such an event. Yet, the day was sunny, promising warmth, and Alessandro, the event coordinator, believed in challenging both one's limits and the elements.

The race was set in a park, but to her dismay, the obstacles weren't housed indoors. The teams gathered outside on the athletic track, a mix of colleagues intentionally formed to foster new connections. Virginia found herself teamed with Gustavo Tomasani, a married manager with a penchant for inappropriate remarks and an overbearing presence.

"How annoying," she thought, noticing his reluctance to be her teammate. Their tensions escalated after a recent hallway confrontation where she put him in his place for his lewd comments. It was an incident she didn't regret; it might have ended his advances.

Alessandro, the coordinator, outlined the race rules. "It's a timed event," he explained. "Each team has a colored bib. You'll start together, tackling three obstacles. First, a lap to reach the initial challenge—a balance beam. Partners must traverse, feet on opposite walls, hand in hand, without touching the ground. If you fail, start over."

Virginia listened intently as Alessandro continued. "Next, a piggyback run. One carries while the other rides. Back to the start, everyone regroups. Lastly, a wooden wall to clear, then the grand finale—mud!" He chuckled. "First team across the finish line wins!"

As Alessandro spoke, Virginia glimpsed Tomasani nearby, his countenance reflecting their recent confrontation. Her strategy to deter him seemed to have worked. Now, the only thing on her mind was conquering those obstacles and leaving Tomasani in the mud—literally.

"I've already forgotten how to deal with the first obstacle..." someone complained.

"Don't worry; we're here too," he pointed to a group of colleagues, chosen to act as referees, "who will follow you step by step, to cheer you on and help you. So, are you ready?"

"Arianna, shall we run together?" asked Virginia to a colleague who nodded to her and they paired up.

The first obstacle was objectively fun. That sort of toblerone-shaped base put them in a bit of a bind, because at first, they put their feet on the ground, a couple of times, but as soon as they understood how to balance their different weights and heights, they embarked on a sort of dance, rocking up and down like on swinging swings until they reached the bottom. They laughed like crazy.

Once the first obstacle was over, Virginia's yellow team was in third place and they began to tackle the second obstacle. Arianna loaded Virginia on her shoulders, because she was very thin, but not being very tall, she couldn't keep her balanced and every now and then they had to stop to get back on. "Saddle up," her co-worker yelled at her and Virginia laughed, because she was obviously sliding backwards. They finished in a fairly decent amount of time, but exhausted. The fact that other coworkers were also taking a long time gave them time to recover.

Finally, having moved on to probably second place, they faced the last hurdle and, as Virginia would find out, the hardest.

"Come on!" Encouraged Alessandro upon seeing her. Virginia grabbed onto the rope and climbed the wall with difficulty. When she reached the top, she slipped back and had to start again.

On the second attempt, desperately clinging on

and helped by a colleague who supported her, she managed to get over the wall and slide down. "Geronimo!" she shouted, but the satisfaction of having overcome the obstacle, immediately turned into discontent because she plunged into a sea of mud.

"Oh, no!" She felt her body cool down in an instant and began to shiver despite being hot from all the running she had done so far. She wanted to get out of that slime and began to trudge by clinging to some taut ropes that emerged from that puddle.

"Ew!" She came alive and pulled with all the strength she had until she could get out of that quagmire. A co-worker handed her a rectangular towel, not very large, and pushed her to the side as others were coming.

She leaned against the tree nearby and tried to wipe her face and hands as best he could.

She heard someone clapping their hands. And that unmistakable, rogue voice saying, "Way to go, Virginia, way to go..."

"Guglielmo?" She saw behind him, but secluded, another man. One of the other four who had been with him the day before.

The cellist approached her, smiling slyly. "If you want to count me in, I had to figure out who you were and what you were capable of. No one can stop you, I guess..."

Virginia tried to wipe her forehead, but she felt the mud was impossible to remove. A few colleagues had begun to recognize the Maestro, she could hear the first chirps. She was still panting and felt embarrassed for him to see her in that state: she was sure she was horrible.

She blushed, because the cellist took the towel from her and began to remove a few bits of congealed mud from her cheeks. She saw a flash across his eyes.

"You know what you remind me of? A women's mud wrestling match I attended a while back..."

"Oh, mud wrestling enthusiast, huh?"

"Actually, no." He grabbed her shoulder and murmured in her ear, "They were fighting over which one of them I'd sleep with. But you, well, you're unrivaled..."

Virginia snatched the towel back, her laughter echoing irony. "Oh, spare me the Latin lover cliché, please. You're not the only man with an instrument in the world." Her shove caught Guglielmo off guard, but he grasped onto the towel, tugging her closer. The momentum threw Virginia off balance, struggling to regain her footing, and in a frantic attempt, she pushed him away, leading both into a direct plunge into the muddy puddle.

Guglielmo ended up on his back, still clutching Virginia, who leaned on his arms for support, their faces now masked in the gooey muck. Neither released their grip on the towel, caught in a soggy standoff.

"Give it here, Maestro!" Virginia demanded, seizing his towel. She wiped at the mud, trying to maintain seriousness but eventually broke into laughter. "Hold on a second... Stop. You've got a bit of slime, right here, on your chin. Just a little, a little bit. Ah, there you go, all gone!" She tossed the towel playfully at him, both of them joining in the amusement. Guglielmo, chuckling, quipped, "Oh, thank you, miss, I couldn't quite figure out what was bothering me."

He wrapped an arm around her waist as they stood, gazing at each other, wordless, their bodies intertwined, trembling not from the cold, but from the shared moment. "Are you okay?" he whispered softly.

"Yes, what about you, are you hurt?" she replied, equally hushed. "I'm sorry, I didn't mean to..."

Several colleagues, including Claudio and Martina, had gathered around the muddy scene. "Virginia, are you all right?" Claudio extended his hand to help her up. "And you, Maestro?"

"Yeah, I'm good, thanks. Just a little stumble, I guess!" Guglielmo scratched his head, pulling himself up, and immediately became the center of attention for a group of admiring women.

"Come on," Virginia said, taking his hand.

"Apart from cleaning you up, I need to rescue you from this swarm of admirers." She smiled and then turned to Claudio with a serious tone. "Would you mind coming with us? I might need some assistance."

The man who had arrived with Guglielmo followed closely behind, and Martina promptly chimed in, "I'm coming too!"

"Yes, perfect!" Virginia responded firmly, feeling Guglielmo's hand, strong yet gentle, guiding her without causing any discomfort. She noticed that the entire SiVery Event had stopped, all eyes fixed on them, including Mister Siveri, the big boss.

But it wasn't the attention that flustered her; it was the surge of hormones seemingly rekindling their storm next to the cellist. She tried to steady herself.

Okay, think business mode! Treat the Maestro like a client! Figure a way out of this mess! Siveri might actually fire me this time!

"Martina, stick with me," she directed with confidence as they entered the facility housing the gym and locker rooms. Taking charge, she continued, "Claudio, could you ensure Maestro Nucci gets towels for a shower?"

"Don't worry about me. Enrico will handle it," Guglielmo assured her, gesturing toward the man while keeping her close. Then he asked, "Once we're cleaned up, would you like to have lunch with me?"

CHAPTER 4.

Emerging from the locker room, Virginia found Martina in a flurry. "The Maestro's outside waiting for you! Hurry!" She was surrounded by other colleagues, a mini-delegation ensuring Virginia made it to meet the Maestro. If she got lost, Virginia was certain one of them would heroically step in and take her place.

"Did the cellist escape unscathed?" Virginia asked Claudio dryly.

"Well, the bodyguard and I had to intervene. Siveri, too," he nodded toward the boss by the exit, "stepped in to calm things down. Luckily, he talked to the Maestro, so the colleagues had to back off. Then the Maestro's phone rang, and he left. Siveri stayed behind, keeping an eye." He chuckled, but Virginia didn't share the sentiment. "So, he invited you to lunch, huh?" he added.

Impatiently, she touched his arm. "I'll go talk to Siveri and explain."

Approaching the boss, she started, "Mister Siveri, I wanted to-"

"Virginia, go on! The Maestro's waiting," he

interrupted her firmly. It was an order, and she knew better than to resist.

Fine, as a final wish before the guillotine, it couldn't be better, she thought, descending the steps toward Guglielmo. He stood by the car, his long coat fluttering in the wind, blond hair tousled, engrossed in a call. Spotting her, he smiled and raised a finger, signaling he'd finish the call soon. He looked dressed up while she wore a jump black suit. Not exactly dressed for the occasion. Her only upscale touches were the blue wool coat cinched at the waist, short above the knee with double rows of gold buttons, and the Chanel strap. She pulled the coat tighter over her chest.

Enrico, the bodyguard, helped her down the last step and opened the door to the sleek black Mercedes with tinted windows. It was a gem, featuring white leather interiors, a smoked glass partition between the driver's seat and the back, and a starry ceiling. It was dazzling.

"Ugh, look at me I look like a mess," she grumbled, glancing down at her sneakers and at her sweatsuit.

"You look perfectly fine, believe me!" Gugliemo chimed in, amused, as he stepped inside, adjusting his topknot and coat. Suddenly, the car was filled with his presence—his scent, his smile, his toned physique.

As the limousine started moving, Virginia pretended to look for something in her purse but it slipped from her grasp, with the contents spilling across the floor. "Damn!"

"Wait, let me help you," Guglielmo offered, collecting her scattered items and passing them back to her. Virginia arranged everything in her purse, finally slipping her glasses into their case. Guglielmo nodded knowingly. "Nearsighted? Me too. I tried tests for surgery, but, you know, the shape of the eyeball and all. Doesn't seem to be ideal for my eyes, so I'm stuck with contacts." He pointed to his iris. "See?" Leaning a tad too close, Virginia thought, I might be nearsighted, but I can see you just fine. You're a hunk. Cheeky, but a hunk nonetheless.

"Oh me too," Virginia shook her head, leaning back further. "I could never do it. I'm too scared! And besides, this way, I'm immune." She adjusted her ponytail.

"Immune to what?"

"To love at first sight, obviously!"

Guglielmo gave her a half-smile. "Oh, really? Love at first sight never happened to you?"

"Never."

Before the car had completely halted, the cellist had leaped out, darting to Virginia's side to graciously open the door for her.

"Have you ever been to Das Loft?" he

inquired, extending his hand to assist her exit the car.

"Um, no…" she replied tentatively.

"The view is spectacular. It's better at night, but we'll have another chance to visit," he mused.

Jeez Maestro, we haven't even had a proper date yet and you're already thinking about our future together?

She felt her cheeks flush and was sure her alert level had risen to Pantone color number 485: fire red.

She looked up first at the wall of the very tall glass building overlooking the Danube and then at her handsome chaperone who was waiting for her, holding the door open for her. "Please," he said, letting her pass. The interior from the lobby was ultra high-tech and from there they took the elevator that took them to the eighteenth floor and when they entered the restaurant, Virginia was overwhelmed by the view of the city that stood out clearly, thanks to the glass windows that seemed to surround her seamlessly. The ceiling was all a play of colors that only increased the feeling of dizziness.

And I still haven't had a drink....

She peered around again and it definitely didn't look like one of those restaurants she could have afforded, especially not the way she was dressed so she turned to Guglielmo and asked him, "Are you sure you want to eat here? I'm not dressed well enough for this place."

"Trust me," Guglielmo assured her, brushing her waist with an open hand. "You look stunning!"

One of the two attendants, motioned to the coats, while the other, pointing toward the tables spoke in German. "*Maestro, wir haben an die Ecke gedacht, so dass Sie eine noch breitere Sicht haben werden. Sie werden den Stephansdom vor sich haben.*"

William replied cheerfully, "*Oh, ja, danke, großartig!*"

Virginia blushed because she hadn't understood anything and took off her coat, with her head down, to give it to the wardrobe attendant. She put the Chanel over her shoulder and, like a warrior, tried to keep a proud posture even if inside she was panicking. The table was in an enviable position: Vienna loomed below and the spire of St. Stephen's Cathedral rose like a spike to the sky.

The waiter moved the center chair for Virginia and William sat on the other side, facing her. Touching her ponytail, she asked, "Can you translate what you said to each other for me as well, please?"

"I told him to bring you a pineapple and green cucumber appetizer." He answered her quietly and opened the menu.

"Ha, ha, ha, very funny." She pondered for a moment, making up her mind about the words she heard, and, eyes wide, worriedly asked, "Ah, so haben werden, does that mean green cucumbers?"

"Ha, ha, ha! No! You do have an ear, though, Virginia. I think you could learn German quickly. I can teach you, if you want..." He used his usual swaggering, shameless tone and Virginia in response, sticking her tongue out at him, said, "Yes, and I'll teach you this one!"

William seemed amused and put the menu down, crossing his powerful arms. He smiled at her. "You're quite a pepper, Virginia."

"Me? You rather! You don't miss a chance to poke me."

"I like that..."

Virginia felt her cheeks grow hotter and her breathing heavier, but she tried to keep calm and asked him indifferently, "And what about your girlfriend? How is she not jealous?"

"What girlfriend?" He brought his face closer to Virginia's, frowning, falsely pouting, and she reciprocated by extending her hand and answering, widening her eyes, "Do you remember? Last night..." and mentally thought: I wasn't the cat meowing on your bed. I wanted to, trust me, but it wasn't me....

Guglielmo touched his chin, ambivalent. His eyes seemed to laugh. "Jealous?"

The waiter arrived and, opening his notepad, said, "*Sind Sie bereit zu bestellen?*"

"*Ja, aber können wir uns auf Englisch*

unterhalten, die Dame spricht kein Deutsch," replied Guglielmo.

"Oh, yes of course, excuse me Maestro, excuse me Miss. I was saying, are you ready to order?"

"What do you prefer, Virginia?" he reached out to her and touched her fingers in a very intimate gesture. She reciprocated and looked back at him and said, "You order, since you know the language. I trust you."

"Mmm, okay... They make a great bread here with butter and basil. A treat." He turned to the waiter, "I am guessing you are going to bring that amuse bouche you usually make. That pan brioche with basil and butter, right? Well then, I'd like some champagne. Dom Pérignon will be perfect. The 2013 vintage of course." She looked at Virginia still playing with her fingers and commented, "I guess you prefer meat right?"

She nodded, touching his thumb with her index finger. He barely retracted, a strange grimace, and Virginia tried to remove her hand immediately, but he gave her an almost imperceptible nod. "Well then, I think we'll go with the gazpacho, they do it particularly well here, and after that a truffle filet and the usual chocolate mousse. Does that work for you?"

"Sure, yeah, everything looks great to me," Virginia replied, gently stroking his thumb.

He smiled at her, returning the caress.

Virginia waited for the waiter to leave and leaned towards him, "I haven't forgotten about the question you asked me earlier, my dear. I don't have a boyfriend, or a ring on my finger, so it's easy for me not to be jealous."

"Any flirtation with one of the co-workers?"

"God no! The HR person must have been short-sighted, like us, or they selected them directly in the swamps of the green orcs. Not even one who is just barely acceptable..." she replied, transfixed.

The cellist's laughter infected her and he continued to chuckle when she added, "Or who even has a sense of humor. In short, a disaster across the board for the entire SiVery organization."

"You really do have a beautiful smile," Guglielmo told her, in a more serious tone.

Oh, God. Is he courting me? That was the first thought and she lowered her gaze.

The sommelier brought the champagne, pouring it into the flutes and meanwhile the waiter served that bread with butter and basil, which, once tasted, sent Virginia into raptures. She ate with her eyes closed and when she opened them again, she blushed because Guglielmo had leaned his head on her arm and was admiring her in a way she thought was indecent. They both drank again without looking away or speaking and Virginia held the flute in front of her eyes, in a vain attempt to defend herself from that provocative sensual attack, only apparently quiet. Only the sound of rising bubbles could be heard, as if it had been that of a thousand tiny bells.

The silence was interrupted by the cellist, who leaned back and began to speak, calmly:

"I've had a lot of women, but only a couple of serious relationships. The last one ended over a year and a half ago. How about you?"

Virginia set the flute to the side and let the waiter serve the first course. "Thank you," she murmured, raising her head imperceptibly as she mentally tacked on her response.

Don't say it, don't say it. Don't talk about Carletto!

She lowered her gaze and mumbled, "Do I have to include Carletto from year two picking his nose?"

There, I said it.

Guglielmo laughed, settling himself better in the square, brown armchair and spreading his arms wide, holding onto the ones he had at his side. He stretched his legs out, until they touched Virginia's.

"By all means, let's include Carletto the nasal explorer!" He continued to laugh.

He's touching me.

"And he even wanted me, afterwards, to take his hand. That hand, those fingers..." said Virginia, squinting and reiterating the last words. "Yuck!"

"Oh, no, come on! I feel like throwing up! Ew!" They laughed together and finally she became serious again. "Including him, five; and no serious relationships. I mean, none that can even be considered..." She retracted her legs.

"So, you just think about working..."

"I compensate for those who only think about something else instead..."

"Someone has to sacrifice, too..." he laughed slyly as he peered under the table and added, "Do you like what you do?"

"Very much so. And I realized that you also really like playing your instrument..." The tone was deliberately mischievous. She enjoyed that moment with him.

"Ha, ha, ha, enough said," Guglielmo returned to find her ankles and at that point she didn't pull away. She intentionally wanted to lose that battle.

"The serious girlfriends, how come they left?"

"And who's to say I wasn't the one who left them?"

"Something makes me believe that you, my dear Maestro, have done something to irritate them."

"And for what reason would you leave me for example?"

"And who says I'd get together with you in the first place, Herr Nucci?"

Guglielmo took the napkin and tossed it to her side. "My dear Miss Ranieri, this is indeed a challenge."

Virginia looked at him defiantly, rubbing her ankle against his.

Challenge accepted, she thought, taking the napkin and, gently wiping her mouth, she gave it back to him with a blatant gesture. He took back the napkin with a bow of the head.

All in all, a little gym time will do me good.

And what a gym, she was facing.

"Ah, look," the cellist brushed her fingers again, beaming. "Earlier, I had a little talk with your boss. Tonight you and he are invited to my concert."

Forget the gym, she thought, this is serious dancing.

Virginia's face widened into a smile.

CHAPTER 5.

For that evening, Virginia wore the sheath dress with a reverse slit, as she called it. Black, like her hair, which she had tied into a bun, adorned with a Bow embellished with glitter. The dress had a cut right down the middle and reached the beginning of the breast. The two flaps still remained straight and almost stuck together, but just in case, she had bought a pin to put in the middle to close that cut. The pin intentionally stayed on top of the coffee table.

She put on her blue coat and ran downstairs, because the boss was surely waiting for her. She had made arrangements with Carolina, who had arranged the cab to take them to the theater and back to the hotel, in time to join the farewell dinner with the other colleagues.

"You look very elegant, Virginia," Siveri told her smugly, seeing her coming.

She smiled; they hadn't spoken yet, and he didn't know how he took the whole thing with Guglielmo.

"The invitation I received today from the Maestro, I must say I was very surprised."

Hopefully you were pleasantly surprised, she thought.

Siveri continued, "My wife, she's been telling me about this cellist for a long time. When I told her that we were seeing him tonight, she asked me to get an autograph."

Figures, even the boss's wife is under the cellist's spell.

"Mister Siveri, I'm sorry for what happened this morning, in front of everyone." She told him, deep down she felt guilty.

"Oh, well, your fiancé certainly livened up our team building event..."

"He's not my fiancé, but yes, I'd say Guglielmo definitely wreaked some havoc." She thought back to all the female colleagues, suddenly going crazy.

They arrived in front of the Vienna Theater, the Staatsoper or sunken casket, which was beautiful at night. The building, illuminated by white lights, vaguely resembled a precious trunk, a jewel box, and had, at the top, like knobs put there to open it, the statues of the winged horses of Erato, which stood out with their blue glow. She was excited, she had never even entered the Teatro alla Scala in Milan and now she was suddenly catapulted into another of the European temples of music.

The stalls were beginning to fill up. "Come,

we are in the first row!" said the Siveri all gloating and pointed to the seats reserved for them.

"Ah, well, just in front of him..." commented Virginia looking down at her heels and taking off her coat.

The lights dimmed and the curtain rose on the four musicians. Illuminated by the lights, with elegant manners, they bowed to the audience applauding them, after which each took his place. One of them, in particular, sat in the only chair placed in the center, exactly opposite Virginia. He adjusted the tails of his suit and placed the cello between his legs. His manner was resolute, his gestures clear. Virginia sensed a certain allure, tightening her grip on the chair's arms.

The violinist standing to the left of the cello nodded to the other two, standing, and the concert began with a classical piece, Bach: Cello Suite No. 1 in G major. The four of them played with earnestness, the acoustics of the hall enveloping the moment in magic. The cello's deep tones intertwined with the violins' soaring high notes, evoking a poignant exchange.

At the end of the piece, the cellist stood up and along with the others made a new bow, inviting for an applause that the audience did not deny. He turned around, rearranging the queues once again, after which he conducted. And the music changed. Literally. Virginia recognized from the first notes,

Roar by Katy Perry. Coincidentally, it was also one of her favorite songs. And it became even more so, because Guglielmo made the music vibrate in her body.

He looked like he was possessed.

The cellist wielded his bow with a commanding force, coaxing it over the strings in an unwavering, relentless motion. The horsehair of the stick fluttered at its ends akin to William's hair—a mane swaying from side to side. Amidst constant movement, his face and body seemed to dance, yet the music remained flawless. He puffed, tightened his shoulders, widened them, displaying fleeting hints of anger, only to transform them into fleeting smiles. His expressions shifted from frowns to rapture, causing the cello to pirouette and then halting it firmly with his legs.

At times, he appeared on the verge of rising, only to lean back against the rest, then immediately spring to his feet, a smile directed at the audience, his posture slightly curved. Holding the bow but not using it, he plucked the cello strings as if they were a harp or guitar. Finally, he would sit, sharply maneuver the instrument, and tap rhythmically on its back, urging the violins to join him in a quest for profound sound, for that perfect note. Even in those brief pauses, his gaze remained fervent, resuming the cello with renewed vigor, moving the bow arm with eagerness while the other hand crafted the notes, leading to the inevitable and resolute conclusion of the music.

The repertoire of contemporary pieces they revisited seemed to have no end and what struck Virginia most was the fact that the tip on which the cello rested was not at all affected by the fervor of those who were playing it.

She, on the other hand, was experiencing that ardor, and how. She was enraptured by the strength, the energy. The beauty, the audacity. She felt again all the sensations she had had the night before, when she had been close to him. She felt that superb body on her. She desired him and blushed.

The concert ended and the lights went up all over the theater. The Four Bows approached the edge of the stage and bowed repeatedly, while the audience continued to applaud and shout the Maestro's name. Someone threw toward Guglielmo red roses, others red hearts and red teddy bears, and, *dulcis in fundo*, even a red bra!

Seriously?

She glanced toward the cellist who was taking a few tributes and bowing to the front and sides, several times. Then she saw him say something toward one of the three violinists who walked away, quickly.

The curtain slowly began to close and a few

women screamed to try to hold him back a little longer. Gugliemo finally said, waving, "Thank you! Good night everyone!"

An usher approached them. "Mr. Siveri? Ms. Ranieri? Please follow me, the Maestro is expecting you."

Virginia was in a panic and a mixture of feelings: she wanted to see him again as much as she intended to stay away from him, because she felt that near him, she was no longer in control.

The usher, drawing aside the curtain of a doorway that gave onto the backstage area, urged them to follow him, "Please come this way," and, once they were near the dressing rooms, added, "Here, if you can wait here. Just a moment and the Maestro will be right out."

Virginia leaned against the wall, arms folded over her light blue coat, while Siveri ventured out into the hallway and began chatting with Enrico, the maestro's driver, in front of one of the many doors. He turned to give her a nod; they were evidently in front of the cellist's dressing room. Virginia sketched a smile and stood staring toward them.

Finally, after a quarter of an hour, the door opened and Guglielmo came out with his usual strong-willed manner, looking left and right. He absent-mindedly greeted Siveri, and as soon as he saw her, he ran up to her, delighted, "Virginia, you're here!"

Oh, how handsome he looked! It wasn't just the face, the physique. It was his bearing, his gait, that Virginia knew corresponded to a sensual and dark voice, to an indomitable nature and a sincere soul. After having seen him play, she knew without fear of contradiction that Guglielmo had a frank, genuine character. His crystal clear laugh was her litmus test and she loved to make him laugh. The smile was the first thing she fell in love with.

Alert Level: Pantone Red, 1663.

The cellist had a towel around his neck and was wearing a shirt that he had not buttoned. You could see the effects of assiduous gym attendance and heavy use of the bow and cello. He gave her a light kiss on the cheek.

"Hello..." she said timidly, peeking under his shirt, a gesture he didn't miss.

"I took a quick shower, otherwise I would have been unpresentable," he pointed to his still damp hair.

Silence, interrupted by the squeak of a woman who emitted a shriek, blurting, "Maestro, wir sind Ihre Fans!"

Several female groupies had appeared out of nowhere.

"*Ach ja, ich komme!* Wait, Virginia..." He seemed annoyed, but he didn't object to the selfies and autographs. At one point there was Siveri as well, which Virginia heard him clarify, "It's for my wife, not for me!"

Once the women were escorted, by force, out of the backstage area, Guglielmo returned to her. Without looking at her, he gently clasped her hand in his own, closed fist, and turned to Siveri, "The next time I play in Milan, you and your wife must absolutely come! As my guests, of course."

"I thank you already, also on her behalf. The concert was very exciting, congratulations, Maestro."

"Thank you, thank you. Did you like it?" He asked Virginia. A hand had rested on her shoulder and Virginia didn't mind that massage, slow, gentle, almost listless. She took a fleeting glance at the white shirt, which opened and closed in time with her breath, and imagined white sheets. And the two of them, in bed.

Cool off your hormones, Virgi! She shifted and coughed.

"Yes, very." She stared at him with wide eyes, trying to convey her thoughts to him.

We can't flirt in front of my boss!

Or was it just her doing it?

She tried not to look at him.

"Well, I'm off then," said Siveri. "I'll stand in for you at our dinner, Virginia, don't worry." Was it her impression or had he winked at her?

Calm down, calm down!

She seemed to calm down, though the thought of letting her boss go did not seem like a good idea.

"Good night," said Guglielmo, "I have your number; I'll let you know when I get my dates set!" As he spoke those words, he held on to the wall where Virginia stood.

He enjoys cornering me, the Maestro.

They waited for Siveri to disappear behind the curtain before speaking, even if it wasn't the words that pierced the air. Guglielmo's fingers moved over the slit in reverse; from the neck, they walked slowly along the slit until they reached the end and when they were there, they lingered. Virginia took his wrist firmly and he retracted it, but she ended up on top of him. He had lifted her a few inches and, she, suspended, held her breath as the black iris and the sea-green iris sought each other in a sinful game of glances.

"I'm hungry, I never eat before a concert," whispered Guglielmo who had not yet set her down.

"Tell me we're not having sausage and sauerkraut."

"Just sausage."

"Oh good, I hate vegans!"

She touched the ground again, but her feet still seemed to fly. They exited the theater. Guglielmo's coat, as a result of his hurried pursuit, waved and ended up on her, between her legs, as they walked quickly back to the hotel. Virginia tried to pull it off, but it was impossible, she always ended up with it between her thighs. And what was worse was that this was exciting her. Guglielmo didn't seem to realize it and she followed him in small steps, holding on with both hands to his arm, imposing, vigorous, and it seemed to her that every now and then, when she bent down to struggle against the flap of wool, he hoisted her a few feet, to make sure she didn't fall behind. The cellist had the gait of a lion, and Virginia felt that she was his prey. The feeling of indecent bewilderment was rising in her throat.

I'm making love to him even before we are in the hotel!

The revolving doors of the hotel gave her pause, but once inside she was once again dragged by one hand, in front of the elevators.

One of the receptionists, as soon as she saw them, hastened to say: "Maestro, here are some letters for you..." but Guglielmo did not answer, looking up, impatient for the light on the ground floor to come on. At the woman's second attempt, he snorted, again without turning around. In a gesture of compassion towards the girl, Virginia waved to her not to insist and at that moment, a customer joined them. Guglielmo blew again from his nostrils, as if he had been a bull waiting to charge the matador and

Virginia felt a shiver run down her back. The elevator doors opened and she felt herself literally spinning inside. She ended up in a corner, while William, facing the automatic doors, stood in front of her, arms outstretched, shielding her, as if the random guest could take her away.

She took advantage of that moment and took off her coat, folding it properly, because she knew she wouldn't have that much time later. With her free arm, she wrapped her arms around his waist. She felt him tremble and squeezed harder.

The man who was with them left at the fourth floor and the cellist, as soon as they were alone, took her hand and kissed her palm, but he did not turn around and continued to stare impatiently at the lights of the floor markers. He already had the room key ready and as soon as the doors opened again, he urged her to follow him without delay to room 501.

Once inside, Guglielmo shed his coat swiftly, discarding it carelessly on the floor before taking Virginia's coat and casually tossing it onto an armchair near the entrance. His urgency was palpable as he initiated a passionate kiss. With practiced moves, he unzipped her dress, sending a thrilling shiver down her spine. His hand slid beneath the fabric, eliciting a soft, satisfied hum from him. As he attempted to remove her hold-up, he abruptly let go.

Virginia watched in wide-eyed surprise as he

swiftly unbuckled his belt, a whirlwind of impetuosity that left her momentarily stunned. Holding her dress at shoulder height to prevent it from slipping, she was taken aback when Guglielmo deftly removed his pants, leaving her standing, dressed only in the dress. In one fluid motion, he lifted her and placed her on the bed, kneeling before her with an unwavering gaze.

Their eyes locked, mirroring the intensity of the moment. Guglielmo pulled her closer, and with an unexpected grace, he lifted her, their bodies intertwining as they continued their fervent embrace. "You're so beautiful," he murmured, the excitement evident in his voice. In a surprising display of balance, Virginia found herself suspended in the air, her legs wrapped around his waist, as they moved together.

As sensations pulsed through her, Virginia surrendered herself to the moment. Her head and arms arched backward, enveloped by a surge of euphoria. Each movement seemed to synchronize with the music that reverberated within her, a crescendo of passion in harmony with their union.

CHAPTER 6.

The flight to Milan, which she had barely managed to catch, had landed very late and she had arrived home when it was already six o'clock in the evening. After what had happened the day before, she had tried as much as possible to avoid talking to her colleagues, but she had felt their eyes on her: the Maestro and Virginia had opened the file.

She knew that many had wondered how she knew him and could have become so intimate with him to the point of throwing him in the mud, having lunch with him and being invited to one of his concerts, unscheduled, but only Claudio had the courage to speak frankly to her.

"Look at you, you're a piece of work. You bring the most handsome cellist in the world to our get-together and instead of making proper introductions, you throw him in the mud in front of all of us! How did you two meet?"

"Oh my God, Claudio. I just know him. Period." She smiled at him.

"I see, you can't tell me more, I guess what happens in Vienna stays in Vienna... however, you know, the fact that you know him..."

And how do I know him.

"From now on you will be the most envied woman in SiVery Events, mark my words."

Once home, she opened the suitcase and removed the bag where she had put the sweatsuit full of mud, throwing it in a corner, and, in its place, she put the bag with the gifts. After that, she took the duffle bag she had prepared beforehand, got into the car and stuck to the plan. She drove non-stop to Casciana Terme in Tuscany. Four hours by car to spend those few days of vacation with her father and the dog. A Golden Retriever, which they had named Birbi.

Even if the thought of Guglielmo did not leave her and in fact, in the car, she could not think of anything but him and those two crazy days in Vienna.

That very morning she had woken up with the cellist's arms and legs pressed against her body, still feeling dizzy from the night that had just passed. She had grabbed her cell phone and had impetuously relieved herself because it was late, abruptly waking up the sleeping beauty.

Like a movie, she retraced those hours.

"Where are you going?" The voice was slurred, but still deeply sensual.

"Good morning to you too..." she strode over to him, but in an agitated voice explained, "I have a plane to catch, I have to hurry!"

Guglielmo cinched her waist and with one leg held her to him. "Stay here, I'll take you back to Milan."

She looked at him in his entirety. He was clearly all awake now.

"I've got to eat breakfast, get dressed, and catch the plane. I promised my father I'd spend Christmas with him. When I get to Milan, I leave for Casciana Terme."

Guglielmo settled in better. "So, I'll drive you to Casciana Terme." He kissed her neck.

She tried to mediate. "We can get together again once the Holidays are over, right?"

"No, I want to see you again right now. Stay here." He pressed harder and it seemed to her that she had no choice, or rather, maybe she didn't want to have a choice.

"All right, Nucci, but this better be quick!"

Guglielmo laughed and started stroking her all over, unhurried.

Heck, I'll miss my plane, she thought. Oh whatever!

When they were done, she was in a turmoil and agitation that made her move jerkily.

"When will I see you again?" he asked her, his Pantone eyes even greener.

"I don't know. What are your plans?"

"I have this event in Dubai, I leave on the 26th..."

"And you're coming back when?"

"The fifth of January."

"So I'll see you for the Epiphany. Perfect day I'd say. The stocking, the broom..." She hinted at a smile and Guglielmo kissed her harder than before, then murmured, "Virginia, I can't last so many days without you..."

Me neither, she told herself, but there was no other way and the lights of the cars whizzing along the A1 highway from Milan to Florence brought her back to reality.

She arrived in Casciana after eight o'clock and when she hugged her father again, it took five minutes to pull away. "Oh, my baby girl, finally, how are you?"

Instinct would have led her to answer that she had made a round trip to paradise, with heavenly music, instead she gave a classic good daughter answer. "Yesterday I got back from my trip to Vienna and everything went smoothly. You know the usual corporate stuff, but nice. I also saw a concert, beautiful!" That was the only mention of the Maestro. The evening passed quietly awaiting the next day, Christmas Eve, which was very important in the Ranieri household. They would put the star on the tree. It was a ritual that had been going on for years, ever since their mother had died. She had become their star.

She stared at the picture her father kept on the mantelpiece, the one of the three of them, where her mother was holding her and she had her little hands around both of their necks. Brief serene moment. Her father had never remarried and had devoted himself completely to his work, his house and his daughter, even though at night she sometimes heard him mumbling in his room. It was kind of why she was reluctant to enter into long term relationships. Or medium, for that matter.

He thought of the Maestro and let out a long sigh. "Phew... with you, perhaps, one might venture..."

She grabbed the leash and on the doorstep, as she was fixing the dog, she yelled out to her dad who was fumbling in the kitchen, "Dad, I'm going to take Birbi out and take a walk around the village, need anything?"

"Um..." the man replied.

At that moment, Virginia's cell phone began to vibrate.

"Dad?"

"No, I don't need anything, it's fine!"

Virginia answered the call, as she left her house and held the dog at bay, "Okay, bye dad! And Birbi, stop pulling! Hello?"

"Hi." Soft, low voice. Him.

"Guglielmo, hello," she didn't expect him to call on Christmas Eve.

"Who is Birbi?"

"Jealous?"

"No, just... curious."

"It's the dog, I'm going out for a walk." She opened the gate. "What are you doing?" She tried to play it cool, as if the night spent with him hadn't touched her in the slightest, as if she'd been the tip of a cello. Intact. Instead, just from hearing the sound of that voice, her soul was in complete chaos.

"I'm taking a stroll too."

"Oh, right. By yourself? Doesn't sound like you, Nucci!" she said jokingly, but the answer pierced her and she leaned against the outer wall of the cottage. She raised her face to the sky as she listened to him.

"Actually, there is a woman too. She's up ahead, I'm catching up to her."

Oh, no! thought Virginia. So many beautiful words, all those kisses, and then... Could she be the one he had the night before? Or a new one? That sucks! It could never work, I knew it.

She continued calmly, "In fact, I thought it was strange, you being alone and all. So let's hear it, where are you two taking this walk?" Her tone was sour.

"Oh, in a quaint little town. Hers."

"Describe to me the lucky lady on duty," and in her mind she specified: if she's not super hot, I'll slice you up!

Birbi pulled on the leash and she walked slowly.

"She's tall."

"Of course she is," she interrupted him pointedly, "for someone like you, it's a minimum requirement. What is she, six foot one?"

Giggle. "No, more like five seven."

"But she's like me then! That's not tall. You have a strange sense of proportion, Nucci..."

"For me it's just the right height. If they're too tall, I don't like them."

"Oh, okay, all right. Just the right height."

By now she couldn't hide her altered voice from the anger that was rising in her, "Anyway, go on. What's the color of her hair?"

"Long, black, with a tail, swinging across her back, and her eyes are dark too, intense. I can't see them from here, but I know for a fact, from her gestures, that they're inflamed right now..."

"I see," she wanted to interrupt that description that was going into a little too much detail. Suddenly a light bulb went on in her head. "Does the poor girl know that you're on the phone with me?"

"No."

"Ah! Then why did you call me, Nucci?" She paused to take a breath.

"Because I wanted to hear from you.... You got into my head, Virginia..."

"You, on the other hand, perhaps the head is the only place you have not entered me." She answered him dryly, but William laughed and whispered to her, "So, is there any chance of seeing you again before the new year?"

If it weren't for all your other women, sure!

She held back and tried to respond compassionately, "You know what they say, hope springs eternal..."

He changed his tone and asked lightheartedly, "After your walk today, what are you doing?"

"Ah, nothing much, lunch with my dad."

Darn, maybe I should have told him I was visiting a very dear *male* friend, whatever, I'm just going to get it over with.

She wanted to end the conversation.

"Speaking of lunch, I have to go-" She interrupted because Birbi began to bark circling around her, the leash getting caught between her legs. "Birbi! Stop it!"

She heard him say: "Hello Birbi! Be good, there, good Birbi! You're a real softie!"

The dog curled up and Virginia widened her

eyes, the phone still in her ear. At her feet, Guglielmo was stroking Birbi, who was rolling over on her stomach, happy for those unexpected cuddles. He was holding a bouquet of flowers and a bottle of wine.

"What are you doing here!" she exclaimed, still stunned.

Guglielmo rose up and towered over her: "I told you I would not have resisted until the new year." He handed her the bouquet of little roses and Virginia, taking them, let herself go back, like a diva, leaning on his arm, which held her firmly, despite the bottle. The cellist kissed her very slowly and whispered: "You have very soft skin, like rose petals, that's why I thought you might have liked them..."

Those green eyes were penetrating and Virginia couldn't tear herself away. The desire to continue kissing him was overwhelming, but she forced herself to stop. She then told him, "They're beautiful. I guess now I have to invite you to lunch to reciprocate..."

"And your father? What will he say?"

"Well, he always wanted a boy..."

"I like you..." he chuckled back at her. He gently rested his mouth on hers, his eyes intent on probing Virginia's soul.

What do I do?

Virginia was in an uproar, upset that Guglielmo was there, with her, on Christmas Eve.

They watched each other as if they had been adversaries; they seemed to be fighting. The goal was probably the same, but the paths were different. Virginia was torn between not wanting to become one of his many and longing to be with him.

She saw out of the corner of her eye the Signora Luisa, their neighbor, looking out of the doorway of her house, and so she freed herself from his grip. "Well of course you like me, I'm a woman." She stared at him languidly, nodding towards the elderly woman. "Nucci, you should know that here we have nosy neighbors who have nothing better to do than observe other people's business all day..." and at that point Guglielmo turned and exclaimed, falsely angry, "What, so I can no longer kiss my girlfriend, now?"

Virginia laughed as she saw Luisa walk back into the house and asked, "Am I your girlfriend now? In that case you should also know the kind of flowers your girlfriend likes..."

"And let's hear it, what are they?" His eyes laughed as he went back to holding her.

"I like courgette flowers," she replied, touching the back of his head lightly. "Fried, with mozzarella inside, but without anchovies. Those are my kind of flowers."

He gave her a gentle kiss, which she returned, as she felt his arms press her back in a vain attempt to make out her body under her winter coat.

"Alright, you convinced me, I'm your girl... And the roses, they're beautiful..." She took his hand and pulled him, turning back, toward home.

"Let's go. So we'll let my dad know you're here for lunch, too."

CHAPTER 7.

During lunch, the father held center stage and Guglielmo seemed at ease, unlike Virginia who felt uneasy about that unexpected sync between the two.

"I still can't get over having you here for lunch, Maestro. I am very honored. The concert you did last New Year's Eve was exciting to say the least, even though I watched it on TV," her dad said and turning to Virginia in disbelief, asked again, "You really didn't know who he was?"

Dad, why do you have to keep pointing that out, geez! thought Virginia, who sketched a wry smile and muttered, "Well for that matter, not even the Grand Master here knew who I was..."

Guglielmo laughed and his father turned to him, "What can I say, Maestro, my daughter has always been uncaring about these things and I think she has no ear for music..."

I'm going to throw the pan at his head!

Mr. Ranieri paid no attention to Virginia's state of mind and continued quietly, "I hope this lasagna is to your liking, Maestro, and in any case, the Brunello you brought is a perfect match in my opinion." He observed Virginia good-naturedly and in return his daughter raised her eyebrows to scold him for making that allusion so shamelessly remarked, but which Guglielmo seemed not to have heard. He continued to eat with gusto. "Everything tasted great, even the prosciutto crudo and the caciotta! Seriously, I haven't tasted food this good in years!"

"Look, Maestro…"

"No, Mr. Ranieri, please call me Guglielmo."

"Only if we can be on a first-name basis and as long as you call me by my first name. Francesco."

Oh God, they look like two best friends… Virginia was disgusted by that idyll, but there was nothing she could do to stop them.

"All right, Francesco!"

Francesco smiled and looked sidelong at Virginia, who rolled her eyes at the turn the conversation had taken. They were acting like old friends and she knew that her father was trying to please the Maestro, because he understood that he could be a potential future son-in-law. And what a son-in-law, at that. She couldn't blame him after all. The last boy she'd introduced him to had been Luca and nothing more after that.

"I was telling you, Guglielmo, that the recipe for this lasagna was taught to me by my mother-in-law. I hope it will be passed down from father to daughter."

"Francesco, are you telling me you made these yourself?!" Guglielmo was incredulous and Virginia's father nodded smugly, while the cellist exclaimed with satisfaction, "Wow! They are so good, they melt in your mouth and the meat sauce is absolutely perfect!"

"Eh, yes, my mother-in-" A knot in his throat prevented him from continuing and he brought his hand to his forehead, to try to stop the commotion and then Virginia was able to intervene.

"Oh, sweet Lord, dad!" she exclaimed altered.

She was annoyed with him, because she understood where he was going, and knowing him, he would get there one way or another, but if they really had to touch that subject, then she preferred to do it herself. In a detached and cold manner, she turned to Guglielmo and explained, "My mother died when I was eight years old, and since she's been gone, my father and my grandparents, my mom's parents, have become very close. You can understand... Later, my grandfather passed away and when my dad, after retirement, moved here, my grandmother lived with him. Until two years ago, when she too passed away..."

She took a forkful of the lasagna, holding back an unexpected sadness. She wasn't ready to tell him everything about her family and suddenly she was assailed by that feeling of miserable unhappiness that she knew well and had learned to manage, but in her own way. Not like this. Not coldly. Not in front of the man who was shaking her soul, turning it inside out.

Damn it, Dad! You and your lasagna! What will Guglielmo think now?

"Oh, I'm sorry," Guglielmo said, and as he spoke those words in a grave but gentle tone, he deliberately moved the chair next to Virginia's and put a hand on her shoulder. He barely squeezed and listened to Francesco, who, after he had recovered, was clarifying, "Thank you, Guglielmo. I chose this house because my sister and brother-in-law live in Casciana. Virginia's grandmother needed to be taken care of, and so the cottage was perfect, also because there was this outbuilding, I don't know if Virginia has already shown it to you... Anyway, I set it up for her, so she could come to visit whenever she wanted, but in the end, she only ever comes at Christmas..."

"Dad, you know that my job..."

"I know, I know. Still, I always hope that one day, you'll come here with your husband and kids and I'll stay in the guest house..." he murmured, staring at Guglielmo.

"Dad!" this time she redirected him in a voice. Frowning. "You know how I feel about family...and stop it, please."

Guglielmo stroked her cheek and tried to interject: "Francesco, I understand you. It's kind of like with my own family. My parents live in New York and are the pivot for us three siblings. My older sister is a doctor, but she's always in Nigeria, my brother lives in Singapore and I'm basically homeless, in the sense that I'm around all the time for concerts, even though I divide my time between Milan and London. In the end we manage to see each other once a year and not always at Christmas, as it happened this time too... Maybe if one of us had a family, children, it would be easier to get together..." He squeezed Virginia's hand, bringing his shoulder closer to hers, squeezing.

"Virginia," Francesco became cheerful again, "show him the guesthouse. Guglielmo, you're staying the night, aren't you?"

The cellist replied bluntly, "Oh no, I can go to a hotel, I don't want to impose-"

"No imposition at all! There's room, there's room! Virginia you'll prepare him the house, won't you?"

Yes, dad, I'll definitely take care of him.

She nodded shyly despite the dirty thought and pushed Guglielmo toward the door, "You know what I haven't asked you yet? How did you get here? Do you have a suitcase?"

They walked out, jackets on and Birbi prancing around the cellist.

"Birbi! Stop it!"

"Leave it, it doesn't bother me... I came in the car and I have a duffel bag. I was hoping you would invite me to sleep but instead your father did..."

"I told you he always wanted a boy..."

The white Porsche 911 was parked a short distance away.

"Wow..."

"Want to take a ride?"

"Don't you want to see where you will be spending the night first?" she asked provocatively. "There is a very nice fireplace too…"

"Ah, yes, yes I would really *love* to see where I will be spending the night and perhaps the afternoon too."

They laughed as they went back, holding hands, to the guest house, which was quite far from the main house, maintaining an appreciable independence and privacy.

Inside, the spaces were divided between the living room, with an open kitchen, the bedroom and the bathroom, which made that mini-apartment comfortable for Virginia's brief Tuscan forays. She had furnished it slowly, to her liking.

"Very cozy..." commented Guglielmo, as Virginia bent down to light the fireplace. She walked around, touching the objects, few in truth, that were arranged on some shelves, a few books. She stroked the pink fleece cover on the sofa, then picked up her cell phone, turned on the speaker and chose Gymnopedie N. 1. Soft piano music. Virginia watched the Maestro as he moved slowly towards her.

"Your father is very nice..."

She smiled and nodded. "What about your parents?"

"What about them?" he said.

"I'm sorry you're not with them this year," she petted him and fixed his forelock, while he fiddled with the wood. "Don't you miss your family at Christmas?"

"I'm used to it, it's been that way since I was a kid."

"What do you mean?"

"Well," his eyes stared dully at her, "my brothers and I didn't often spend Christmas together with our parents. For as long as I can remember, maybe it happened four, five times at the most."

"Oh, I'm sorry to hear that," Virginia reached up and hugged him, and Guglielmo sank his face into her belly. "How come?"

"Too complicated, hard to explain." He replied.

"Well," she declared jovially, trying to gloss over the question she had asked, which was in fact too indiscreet, "in this house we celebrate, and will always celebrate, Christmas all together! There is no question about that! I am uncompromising!"

"If you're all about family, why don't you want kids?"

He held her close and she ran her fingers through his hair, pondering the answer.

"Is it because you lost your mother so soon? Because don't you want the same thing to happen to your kids? Is that why you're on the pill?"

"And how do you know about that?" She took hold of his face and lifted it, staring in bewilderment into his eyes, which at that moment had again lost their usual vigorous edge to give way to flashes of shyness.

"The other day when we were in the car and everything fell out of your purse..."

There, that's it, Nucci one, Ranieri zero. And it also explains why you went relaxed, with me....

Despite her thoughts, Virginia said nothing and knelt down again. She picked up a log and placed it in the fireplace. His hands covered hers and she let him. She turned to look at him and murmured, "Your fingers, do they hurt when you play?"

Guglielmo nodded. This time it was he, who had been caught off guard. "And how did you figure that out?"

"The other day," she smiled, "you were playing with my hands, but every now and then you'd make a slight grimace. What about your shoulders?"

"Yes, they hurt too."

"So, Nucci, you definitely need a good massage," she told him, lighting the match and throwing it on the wood, which caught fire immediately. She put on the spark guard, stowed her glasses and grabbed Guglielmo's wrists. Her voice came out persuasive. "Come, Maestro, stand here on the couch. Let me see what I can do for you. My father, many years ago, had a bad bursitis in his arm and I used to accompany him to the physiotherapist. During the sessions, I learned a bit of the art." She placed herself on the backrest, feet on the seat, tapping against the backboard. "Come here!" A smile of encouragement, and as Guglielmo settled in, she lifted his sweater, beginning a slow, circular massage over his shoulders. He took it off completely, remaining shirtless, and then she slipped behind him, continuing to massage him, gently. She studied his moles, his imperfections, and every now and then she kissed a spot on him, lips leaning in, brushing the skin with her cheek. Guglielmo had abandoned himself to those caresses and was leaning forward, head down, emitting short moans of pleasure, his body crossed by shivers.

"Are you cold?"

"No...keep going, please don't stop..."

The music on her phone had now turned to Ravel's Bolero.

"Why did you start playing the cello?"

"Which version do you want?"

"Why? Do you have more than one?"

"Well, I have an official one."

"And that would be?"

"I'll spare you all the corollary and get straight to the point." As if he were repeating a script he said, "Impressed by a concert by the best cellist in the world, Rostropovich, Guglielmo Nucci began playing the cello, at a very early age."

"Nice. And the truth?"

Guglielmo remained silent for a while.

"Do you know that this episode, I've never told anyone about it? Only my brothers, Beatrice and Giorgio, know about it." He tried to touch her and she hugged him.

"I was five years old. My grandmother, Vittoria, was a violinist. A good one, too. When she was young, she had performed for a time at La Scala in Milan, a few concerts. At some point, she had gotten it into her head that we should learn to play the violin, as well as the piano, but unlike my siblings, I was a rebel..."

"And you still are, Nucci," she ruffled his hair and Guglielmo laughed. He became serious and explained, "I still remember that day. I was in the middle of the room, my brother and sister were diligently executing, Grandma was sitting there listening and correcting. At one point, I was so frustrated that I had to hold the violin with my chin, that I threw it on the floor, hard. It ended up across the room and broke." He chuckled. "I still remember with bitterness the piece that Grandma was teaching us. Since then, I have not been able to listen to it. It was sonata number 21 with three violins by Giovanni Gabrieli," he hesitated and added, "I don't think you know it..."

Virginia replied with a frown, pinching his arm, "And who doesn't know Gabrieli?" Guglielmo turned around pleasantly amazed, "Really? You know the sonata?"

She answered nodding very seriously and specified: "Of course I do! And of course I know Gabrieli. Just the other day I ran into him and said, switching to a Roman accent: "Giovà, you know that if you play a sonata for three violins Nucci will get pissed off. He only plays one instrument and-"

Guglielmo turned around, falsely angry. He grabbed her arms and landed her on the couch, while Virginia, trying in vain to defend herself and laughing like crazy, crying out for forgiveness: "God, I'm so sorry, sorry, I could not resist, you were so serious! Ha ha! I had absolutely no idea who Gabrieli was."

"You know what you need from me now?" He abandoned himself on top of her, trying to kiss her.

"No, wait, wait! I really want to know how you came to play the cello!" She shrugged off

William's topknot as he lifted himself up, holding onto his elbows. He stared at her, with his intense green eyes, focused on hers, and went back to telling.

"Grandma took the violin, set it aside, and picked me up. She finished teaching Giorgio and Beatrice, after which only she and I went to a store." He stopped and looked away. He searched his memory. "You know I can't actually recall the whereabouts?"

"In my opinion," Virginia answered him affectionately, continuing to stroke his hair, "it will have been the most beautiful music store you've ever set foot in."

He kissed her and said again, whispering, "Actually, yes, you're right. It was beautiful. There was everything. Pianos, guitars, all the wind instruments. Strings. It was amazing! I wasn't nearsighted yet... It was beautiful. My first cello. I still have it... And Grandma taught me how to play it.... When she died, five years later, I swore to myself that I would become the best cellist in the world."

"And you have become the best cellist in the world. Tell you what, Nucci. Tonight, you're going to put the tree-topper on the Christmas tree. Let me explain. It's a tradition in the Ranieri household and..."

"Explain it to me later. In the meantime, Ranieri, start worrying about this other pointy topper..." he laughed slyly.

"Oh, oh, oh, Nucci..."

They explored each other tenderly, cherishing the intimate connection between their bodies. Guglielmo would pause intermittently, studying her with a gaze that seemed to delve beyond the physical, seeking the depths of her soul. In response, Virginia peppered him with kisses, brushing his nose, tracing his cheeks and the edges of his mouth, while whispering sweet, reassuring words. Her hands caressed his head, his shoulders, the expanse of his back.

Wrapped in each other's embrace, time seemed to fade away. Virginia released soft, contented sighs, feeling the weight of his relaxed body resting upon hers. It was as if he had found sanctuary in her arms, seeking solace after navigating through tumultuous waters.

After they finished, Guglielmo turned once again to her and asked: "So what's the story with the tree-topper?"

"Ever since Mom died, every year at Christmas we put up the star in her honor. This year, I want you to put it up, for your grandmother... I know, I know... maybe I shouldn't have told you. It's personal. I'm sorry. Forget it, bad idea..."

She squeezed him tighter, but Guglielmo said, "It is a very sweet thought and I am honored to take part in the Ranieri family ritual. But your father, he may not be pleased..."

"Oh, on the contrary, he's going to be so happy. I told you, didn't I, that he has..."

"...always wanted a boy...yes you told me. Don't you have male cousins?"

"No, my mom was an only child and my dad's sister didn't have any kids and, oh God..." Virginia covered her face.

"What's wrong?"

"Nothing, it's just that I'm already dreading what's going to happen tomorrow, with the whole Ranieri family. You have no idea, poor thing. You're still in time: run away while you still can, I promise I won't be offended!"

"Ha, ha, ha, I would never run away from you. Ever. You'll see, everything will be fine."

And it all went really well, because, despite his fame, the cellist, strangely enough, had withstood the impact with the Ranieri family in a commendable way. Not even she was as good as him at juggling uncles, cousins and *tombola* marathons. And from someone as famous as Guglielmo, she would not have expected such a humble attitude, which he had demonstrated to possess.

It was clear that on Christmas Day, as soon as the family recognized the Maestro, there was a general uproar, with requests for photos, autographs, and anecdotes, which led everyone to sit in a circle around him in religious adoration, while he spoke. However, the next day, during the classic St. Stephen's *tombola* at his aunt and uncle's house, Guglielmo had now acquired the status of one of the family, to be asked, with sappy looks, to pass the salt or oil. Zia Dora had even gone further, and with the plate in her hand in mid-air, trembling from arthritis, had asked Guglielmo: "Young man, can you put some more peas on my plate?"

Virginia would have liked to hide from the embarrassment, but Guglielmo, not at all annoyed, had gotten up, had taken the plate and had elegantly served the peas to her aunt, who had given him a smile with the few teeths that remained.

In the living room, they had then reached the tipping point, when another aunt, Zia Teresa, had given Guglielmo her dead husband's guitar and blatantly asked him if he could dedicate one of his performances to her, as if one instrument was the same as the other.

"Zia", Virginia interjected decisively, "Guglielmo can't play, doctor's orders, because in two days he starts a series of concerts, if not, he gets tired, you know how it is..." She had made up that excuse right then and there, and tempers had immediately calmed down at the mere mention of a health issue in the great Italian tradition. If this had saved Guglielmo from an unscheduled performance, the older ladies had gone wild in illustrating to the musician their problems related to bad feet.

William listened attentively to the old aunts, bestowing smiles and even caresses, and they had come dangerously close, like moths to the light. At that point, Virginia had decided it was time to stop that torment. With another little lie, combined with military tactics, she had Bowered over to Guglielmo and pulled him from the siege. Taking him by the chest and glaring at the comrades, she had peremptorily asserted, "That's enough, the Maestro must go and rest!" Guglielmo had followed her, bidding farewell with great nods to the old women and relatives, who, fearful of Virginia, had remained seated with sad and melancholy faces.

When they were safely in the guesthouse, she told him, relieved and satisfied that she was able to get away from the family, "I almost lost you in the geriatric ward there..."

"Ah... ha, ha, ha. No, that's not true. Your aunts were all very nice. They reminded me of when I used to visit my grandmother's sisters."

"Mmm, I hardly recognize you. Nostalgic are we now?"

Guglielmo had hugged her from behind, hands all over her. "It feels so good to be with you." It had been at that moment that the cellist had upped the ante, surprising her, in no small part.

"Come with me to Dubai."

"Excuse me?"

"We're leaving in an hour."

She had widened her eyes. "Are you... crazy?!"

"Yes, about you."

"But I must go back to the office! And then I don't even have the right clothes," and while she protested in words, she had retrieved her duffel bag and opened it in front of him: "See? I only have the suits I had in Vienna and that I brought simply because I arrived in Milan late and didn't have time to organize otherwise. In a few days, theoretically, I should go directly to the office from here; in addition, I only have sweatsuits. See?" she told him, slipping them in bulk and zipping them up, hard. She had parried in front of Guglielmo and concluded by saying, "What if I don't have my passport with me?"

"You've got it. I know you have it." His eyes chuckled.

"What if I don't have it?" Arms folded, foot tapping on the ground.

"Go say goodbye to your father," he said, kissing her on the cheek. Then he added: "I saw it when you checked in for Vienna. You had a passport instead of an ID card."

Oh, this is a nice surprise... Did you already

have your eye on me before you got on the plane, Maestro?

      "By the way," the Maestro went on, whispering, "do you have the tailleur from that day, the one with the little gold buttons on the side? You looked particularly nice..."

CHAPTER 8.

And it was precisely the tailleur with the little golden buttons that Virginia was wearing, while Guglielmo was driving the Porsche, in an unconscious way, making the engine scream with rage and changing gears almost always to the limit. The speed was definitely out of the limits, not highway, but human. And that's because, according to Virginia, Guglielmo was driving distracted. He had cranked up some obscure eighties band, which, truth be told, Virginia knew next to nothing about (music wasn't exactly her forte and she did catch the irony in all this), and it blared throughout the car. And when Guglielmo wasn't busy switching gears, his right hand rested on Virginia's knee, with the intention, not exactly hidden, of climbing up her skirt.

"Eyes on the road, Nucci..." she tried to rebuke him, during the last foray.

In response, Guglielmo turned to her, shaking his head to the music and singing loudly.

"Well, bravo, not only do you play the cello, you also sing. But you also might want to watch the road! And slow down, for God's sake, you've already proven your masculinity in other circumstances!"

She took his hand and moved it back to the steering wheel and Guglielmo, laughing, decided to slow down. "You're even more beautiful when you're angry, you know that?"

"Yes, yes, you don't get away with a few pretty words! What's wrong with you? I'm not angry, I'm ticked off is what I am!" Arms folded, she stared straight ahead, the noise of the engine and the music together. "It's getting dark and you're driving like a madman.... What time's our flight? I was better off staying home..."

Guglielmo grabbed the back of her head and said, "I'm not crazy, I'm happy...that's all!"

"And suicidal, too." She shook her head.

"Come on, give me a smile, please, one of those Ranieri smiles, the casual kind, like one of the very first ones you gave me, when we first met..."

"Can I remind you that it was only seven days ago," she answered him dryly. She continued impassively, "The way you talk about it, it seems like it's been a century...and then I have no idea what circumstance you're talking about."

He tried to caress her, but she resisted and, annoyed by Guglielmo's behavior, said: "You have a strange perception of reality, Nucci. Heck, the further I get with you, the more I find out you're a mess, it's going to take a lot of time to fix you."

"In seven days, you've done a lot, Ranieri, trust me..." The hand back on the thigh, directly.

"You settle for little." The fingers slid higher and Virginia didn't flinch.

Guglielmo commented: "Arrived!" and Virginia wasn't sure to which destination he was referring to. Much to her relief, she saw the entrance to the Florence international airport. Guglielmo went directly to the private flights terminal.

"Private? What does that mean?" she asked curiously, but Guglielmo was already talking to Enrico who was waiting in front of the terminal.

"Is everything ready?" the Maestro asked and then added pointing to Virginia, "For her too?"

"Yes, sir," Enrico replied, impassive, and without adding anything else he led the way to the entrance, where a hostess invited them to get into a limousine.

Virginia was bewildered. "Wow, what's this? First class?"

Guglielmo put an arm around her neck and rested his head on her shoulder. "Did I tell you I like your perfume?"

"Oh, thanks, but I didn't put it on..." She felt the same awkwardness again as the first few days she had met him.

"In fact, it's your scent. It's so good. Did you know that scent is the first of our senses to be activated when we are attracted by another person?"

"Okay, Professor Nucci. We're not going to do this for the whole flight are we?"

"Well, since you asked..." he replied laughingly.

The limo in the meantime had pulled up in front of a shiny white Gulfstream.

William took her hand and they got out of the car. She slowed down, she had never been on a private jet before. The ladder was down and a female flight attendant (a bit too attractive for Virginia's taste) was there to greet them.

"Welcome Mister Nucci and Miss Ranieri."

They know my name already? Wow, She thought.

"Good evening," said Guglielmo, "how soon can we take off?"

"As soon as you're ready, Maestro." The stewardess followed them and continued talking. "The clothes you ordered are in the bedroom, while the rest of the luggage is already in the cabin. We also have been lucky to find the 2013 Dom Perignon as per your request."

"Great, we have everything then. Let's take off."

The one who really took off was Virginia. She followed Guglielmo, who had to duck to get into the Gulfstream's cabin, and when it was her turn, she was left speechless. The heels, they moved on the soft, warm cream colored carpet. She whispered to herself, looking at the floor, "The 1306, or if you will... no, no, I think it's really Pantone beige 1306..."

"What did you say?" he asked her, also scanning the floor. "Have you lost something?"

"Ah, no, no," she replied shyly and gazed in wonder at the area where she had landed. The kitchen overlooked a very minimal, but cozy little living room. With regret, she could not dwell on the details, because Guglielmo had already crossed the threshold of the area reserved for them, aft. Virginia ran her hand along the smooth walls that alternated white and brown, giving a very intimate effect, while all the leather seats in the lounge were white. On the coffee table, a light blue vase with fresh roses broke up the immaculate dominance and recalled the blanket of the bed that could be seen at the end, in the adjoining room.

"There is a bedroom, too?" she exclaimed with some emphasis, and stopped on the threshold, leaning against the doorframe: she dared not go deeper than she had already done. She was already satisfied that her blue coat matched that unbridled luxury and she could have traveled upright, admiring that style, until she arrived.

The plane moved and Guglielmo called out to her, "Have a seat, we're about to take off and I need to make a few calls beforehand."

Before what? Before that...? On the plane?

She blushed at the thought.

After the commander's croaking voice had announced the take-off from the intercom, she stood up, adjusting her skirt. Guglielmo took her hand to hold her, continuing to talk and frowning. He tilted his head, grimacing to see if she needed anything.

"Just looking around," she whispered in his free ear and left, going through the door that divided the private room from the rest of the Gulfstream's cabin. She then came back and looked at Guglielmo, with a mischievous look. He was still on the phone. "Still on the phone?" she asked innocently but then took a fresh strawberry and put it delicately in her mouth.

She smiled slyly when she heard him say: "I'm sorry, I have to go. I'll call you back."

Guglielmo put away his phone and gave her a questioning look. She grabbed his hand in hers and pulled him towards the back of the jet, to the private bedroom. He followed her without saying a word.

The room was warmly lit with soft yellow lights, lending it an inviting atmosphere. Virginia turned towards him and smiled wickedly as she slowly walked to the bed that was placed at the center of the room. She then whispered something inaudible into Guglielmo's ear and winked before sitting down on the bed.

Guglielmo nodded and closed the door behind them. He seemed to be in a trance as he walked over to her, only able to make out a few of her seductive words that were laced with desire. He lost himself in her gaze as he stood in front of her and leaned down slowly, until their lips were almost touching. Then, with a deep sigh, they started undressing each other, their desire quickly escalating.

Guglielmo's hands glided over Virginia's body as he slowly and carefully removed her clothes, revealing her glowing skin beneath. His touch was gentle yet passionate; sending shivers down her spine and making her heart race faster with anticipation. Meanwhile, she couldn't help but admire his strong physique and sculpted muscles that seemed to have been carved from marble. Thank God for cellists! she thought.

The intensity of the moment was palpable as they embraced each other tightly in a passionate embrace, exploring every inch of each other with their eager hands. They rolled around on the bed in a playful manner, kissing and moaning softly as they teased one another until finally coming together in an intense union of passion and pleasure that left them both exhausted yet completely satisfied.

CHAPTER 9.

After their high-flying 'session', Virginia glanced down at the outfit Guglielmo's assistants had chosen for her; a beautiful black silk dress, with a light crepe satin that clung to her body in a way she had never experienced before. The finishing touch was an elegant pashmina of pastel pink - the same shade as the Bulgari purse that had also been provided. How on earth did the Maestro's mysterious fashionistas manage to find those matching colors? She wondered.

Guglielmo was also dressed to perfection, with a classic cut suit and, you guessed it, a pastel pink tie of the same exact nuance as her shawl and her purse.

While she was still in awe of the flawlessness and sophistication of the Maestro's organization, Guglielmo had suddenly become tense, almost anxious. He had gone back to the front of the cabin and was nonstop on the phone.

As the Gulfstream began its descent toward Dubai, the city emerged like a jewel amidst the vast desert expanse. Virginia's breath hitched as she leaned closer to the airplane window, her eyes widening in awe at the sight below. Towering skyscrapers pierced the sky, their glassy surfaces reflecting the golden hues of the setting sun. The iconic Burj Khalifa stood tall, casting its shadow over the bustling streets below. The city glimmered with a myriad of lights, transforming the landscape into a mosaic of vibrant colors against the twilight.

As the flight attendant swung the door open, Guglielmo, standing tall with an air of determination, grasped Virginia's hand and whispered, "Promise to stay by my side, always." His grip tightened, a silent plea laced with urgency. The balmy breeze of Dubai enveloped Virginia, bringing with it a distinctive scent—a blend of pink pepper and orange blossom, unmistakably Opium by Yves Saint Laurent. The fragrance lingered in the air, a pervasive presence that seemed to cling to every corner of the jet. And Virginia Bowered where or better yet, *who* was the source of such wonderful scent. She did not need to look too far.

At the end of the staircase, in fact, waiting for them, was a woman, or rather a candidate for Miss Universe in Virginia's eyes who, clipboard in hand, was staring at them with a goddess-like look.

The woman had shiny, jet-black hair meticulously styled with gel, creating a sharp side part that neatly framed her face. Two sparkling hairpins adorned the sides, a shimmering echo of the pearls in her necklace. Her dress, a stunning shade of crimson, cascaded down in a graceful sweep, adorned with sleeves and a modest front slit, barely held together by a single pearly button.

And she was tall, very tall. More or less like the Maestro, she thought.

And then there was her face—piercing blue eyes, a refined French nose, and lips that were full and inviting. Her eyebrows, elegantly straight and meticulously shaped, prompted Virginia to instinctively reach up, attempting to perfect her own in a futile gesture.

She'd seen the woman before, in one of the numerous photos where Guglielmo was always seen with some member of the opposite sex. But Virginia hadn't the faintest clue who she might be. Nevertheless, the woman seemed quite familiar with the Maestro; she approached him, lightly touching his shoulder and inquired, "*Olá querido, como foi tua viagem?*"

"*Fale Italiano, Adriana.*" He replied dryly and continued without looking at her, towards the limo that was waiting for them.

Seriously, Nucci, you even speak Portuguese? What language don't you speak? I don't know Portuguese but the word querido, I definitely understood... What's the deal here, Maestro?

Adriana, walking at the cellist's side, continued to speak, and had switched to an impeccable Italian and Virginia, on the opposite side, peeped out, so as not to miss the dialogue.

"His Excellency has arranged a welcoming ceremony for you and we are expected at the Bulgari Hotel. He has another engagement, so he won't be there and.... Guglielmo, she was not expected. I told you not to bring one of the usual ones. There will be reporters, you know." As she said the last words, she gave Virginia an annoyed look.

Oh, how nice of her... sure just pretend I'm not here, it's the oldest of tricks.

In the meantime, Enrico had opened the car door and Guglielmo had turned to Adriana, motioning for Virginia to get in. With a sneer he exclaimed, "You can take the other car, Adriana. Our patron couldn't care less which of the *usual* women I bring, and all the more so since he won't be present, so she's coming with me, as I had already made you aware."

Ouch! Virginia 1, Adriana 0, she thought as she snuggled into the limo.

"Oh, one last thing" Guglielmo said, "have János, Tamas, and Cori arrived yet?"

"Yes."

"Good; what about the practice room?"

"Yes, it will be available starting tomorrow." Adriana answered him and from the tone, Virginia could tell she was not happy. "Guglielmo, you know that tonight Antonio and I will also be there."

"Fine, so I'll see you there."

The Bulgari Hotel was located on an island, Jumeirah Bay, about twenty minutes from the airport. During the drive Virginia remained silent, nor did Guglielmo do anything to speak, although he continued to hold her hand.

They were both soaking in the view with their windows lowered, letting in the cool desert air. The sun had lowered and Dubai at night was a spectacle and the gazes practically jumped from skyscraper to skyscraper without interruption. The twinkling was reflected in Virginia's eyes, but she couldn't help but be distracted by the reckless motorists who were speeding past in their limousines, often very, very close to her door.

They came to a bridge and saw, below them, the waterway with boats moored on both sides.

"What is it?" she asked without turning around. William approached her without touching her. "It's the creek and those are the boats for tourists. Do you like Dubai?"

"It's very beautiful. Busy, but beautiful."

The resort was even more enchanting, as magnificent were the yachts moored in the roadstead that contributed, with their illuminations, and the consequent reverberation in the water, to increase the glittering effect.

The reception overlooked the bay, and Virginia, wrapped in her pashmina, felt like she was stepping into a grand Hollywood entrance, all nerves and excitement as she entered alongside Guglielmo. The wooden floors and wicker chairs lent a natural warmth to the setting, while a string of small lights hung overhead, enhancing the scenic view of the bay and the brightly lit skyline in the distance. The central space was already filled with groups of people, engaged in lively conversations and holding glasses. Soft music floated in the air.

"Coriolan!" Guglielmo's face lit up with genuine delight. "Cori! How have you been?"

"All good, thanks! We got here this afternoon. And you?" Coriolan replied, casting a nod toward Virginia.

"We just arrived. Meet Virginia. This is Coriolan, Cori to friends. One of the other Four Bows."

"Ah, one of the violinists. Impressive, congratulations." Virginia extended her hand, offering a warm smile. She had recognized him from the photos scattered across websites dedicated to the Four Bows. The man, slightly shorter than Guglielmo and younger, lacked the same athletic build.

"Violist, to be precise. I play the viola," Coriolan clarified before turning once again to the

Guglielmo. "Tomorrow, what time do you want to rehearse?"

"How about in the morning? I'd like to be free in the afternoon ..."

"Ah, that's fine with me. Jelena wanted to do something too... There she is."

"Jelena, hello," Guglielmo greeted her and again introduced Virginia. "Jelena is Cori's wife. A saint of a woman, as I don't know how she can deal with this man every day..." He laughed.

"Hey! What do you mean? I'm the saint of the two!" protested Cori.

The woman grimaced and spoke directly to Virginia. The Italian was correct, but the accent, as well as the name, betrayed a different origin.

"A little notoriety and these guys think they've got the world at their feet! Don't be fooled, dear. Coriolan still believes that children magically dress themselves in the morning..."

Virginia laughed softly.

"Did you bring them?" asked Guglielmo and gave Virginia a fleeting glance.

Nucci, every time the topic of offspring comes up, you look at me.

"Ah, no, Guglielmo! I'm officially on vacation!" replied Jelena. "While you guys are working, I'll be at the spa relaxing and enjoying myself, free of the three little Kovác devils."

"Oh, there's Tamas and János!"

The two men announced by Coriolan approached smiling and the four of them hugged each other with big pats on the back.

Real alpha males...thought Virginia.

A woman approached asking for an autograph and the small group moved towards other fans who, shyly, began to talk to them. Jelena disappeared towards the buffet and Virginia remained near a wicker chair, contemplating whether to sit or wait upright for the Maestro's return.

The air suddenly became scented with Opium.

Miss Brazil at 9 o'clock.

Virginia just turned around and out of the corner of her eye followed the crimson dressed beauty who was approaching with a very hurried pace.

"Are you enjoying yourself dear?" Adriana asked her as she arrived, and she countered, without looking at her, "Are you?"

"Poor thing, you don't think Guglielmo is really interested in you, do you?"

Here we go, the war has officially begun, but yes let's play it straight. Either way, she didn't intend to give her the satisfaction. "Well he is certainly no longer interested in you, that's for sure!" She rebutted.

A nervous laughter shook Adriana in an inelegant way, bending her forward.

"Oh dear me, you absolutely have no idea! I've seen plenty of little women like you come and go with Guglielmo."

"Little woman, my a##!" Virginia clarified, voice firm.

What a first class b$&ch! she thought.

"But that's what you are, dear. You're the last of many and you'll soon be replaced. Has he given you the surprise yet? The one you thought might turn into something serious?"

Imperceptibly, Virginia moved her head and lips, and the Brazilian noticed. She stepped in front of her, grinning wickedly as she said, "Ah, good, she's already done that... so you're at step one. Good girl. Usually, it takes a little longer, one, two months. I'm surprised, but he's probably just more in the mood than on other occasions."

She knows how long we've known each other.

"And if I'm not mistaken, he's already given you the runaround about the origin of his passion for the cello. The next step will be the serenade, just for you. You, him, maybe naked, and his instrument. Melodious sex, trust me. So then you get to step number three, a major gift. For example, a pendant, or a necklace." Adriana touched her cleavage where a trinket dangled, and Virginia didn't miss the gesture.

"After that it's up to you, if he really isn't tired already, then maybe a trip together, otherwise you can start saying goodbye. Make the most of this time, but don't think for a moment that it's going to last."

She walked away, determined, tapping her heels on the wooden floor, toward a small group of people chatting happily and abandoning Virginia to the bitterness of those revelations.

The fact was that, deep down, Virginia knew that the virago might even be right. She herself had seen the effects of Guglielmo on women, and that night in Vienna, when she had shown up, unannounced, in front of his room, he was already busy, probably with one of the many.

She pulled out her cell phone and took a picture of the little group. Adriana was turned towards her. She enlarged the image on the woman's face, saved the changes and posted the photo on her friends chat group, writing only two words: who is she?

The answer came immediately from Sara.

'It's the cellist's ex, the agent, the one I told you about! Where are you? A party? Are you with him? YOU'RE WITH HIM???????? YOU DID IT!!!! You go girl!'

The cell phone vibrated. Sara was calling her. She ignored the call and answered the message concisely, but explicitly to all questions.

Ah, okay... Dubai. And Yes to all questions. As she had foreseen, the cell phone came alive with a life of its own, but she closed everything and put it in her purse. She stayed and watched the virago and a little farther away Guglielmo, who was laughing with Cori and the others. She felt that this world was probably not hers and that the Maestro would never become the man of her life.

A shame.

The cellist came near her carrying two flutes. "Here I am, sorry. I made it." Delivery of the glass and hand on arm. Virginia sipped.

"Would you like to dance?"

I'm already doing that, aren't I? Ever since I met you in Vienna! Oh Jeez... why, why did I let myself go with you...

She looked him in the eye and replied instead: "Yes, by all means, let's dance."

CHAPTER 10.

The next morning, Virginia awoke, her head resting on Guglielmo's arm as he softly snored. She carefully shifted, trying not to disturb him, and tiptoed around the hotel room, which was more like a sprawling mansion. This realization had struck her the night before when they returned late, greeted by the vast living space. Red leather sofas formed a horseshoe in front of a colossal glass window that overlooked the illuminated swimming pool outside. Guglielmo guided her through the home theater into a hallway leading to one of the bedrooms. "I prefer this one, even if it's smaller," he explained, gesturing toward the room. It was snug and rectangular, with wooden walls continuing the villa's theme. At one end lay a bathroom with an expansive white marble shower, a feature that particularly caught her fancy.

"Very nice..."

"Come on, let's go to sleep."

Instead, thanks to the fact that they were undressing in the walk-in closet behind the bedroom, they had made love practically inside the cabin, of which Virginia had appreciated the very large mirror.

As she kissed him she said thoughtlessly, "In our house, I'd really like a cabin like that, with this mirror..."

Guglielmo had caressed her and whispered softly, "Your wish is my command, Your Highness..."

She laughed softly as she thought back to that sincere exchange, which calmed her down a bit, as she was still reminiscent of the Brazilian virago's sour words.

Recalling that moment of the night, she walked barefoot appreciating on her skin the warm feeling of the parquet floor. The great hall was illuminated by the strong light of the morning sun and the long chandelier, above the equally long dining table, seemed to be composed of a thousand pearl necklaces all rolled up and glittering. She felt like one of those divas whose pictures were scattered on the shelves. She went out for a walk by the pool and passed it, descending a marble staircase and finding herself directly on the beach of the bay. The light was bright, the sand soft. Virginia was happy.

A voice brought her back to reality, "Good morning princess, did you sleep well?"

She turned around and saw the Maestro in all his glory. He was clearly very awake.

"Yes, I slept very well, Nucci. But something tells me you're not very interested in my sleep..."

"How did you guess?" he asked with a

provocative grin.

Insatiable, she thought, while laughing. She then went quickly back inside.

After another hour passed, Guglielmo looked at the watch and got up hurriedly from the bed.

"Ouch, I am going to be late!"

"For what?" asked Virginia.

"For the rehearsal. Cori always gets pissed off when I get to rehearsals late. Which happens all the time," he said laughing. Then he looked at her, glowing in the sunlight and added: "Oh God Virginia, where have you been all my life?"

She smiled and gave him a sweet kiss.

***

The Four Bows had the rehearsal set for eleven o'clock, in a recording room located in front of the Palm Jumeirah, the palm-shaped island, which, unlike the Staatsoper, had been built by two Dutch companies.

"And in this case, no one committed suicide," Virginia murmured, as they arrived.

"Suicide?"

"Forget it, inside joke..."

Muffled environment, green and dark orange walls, framed posters of singers and playbills hanging here and there. Even a guitar. They went down a few stairs and the Four Bows settled into the recording room, while she took a seat on the small sofa in the adjacent room. Guglielmo caressed her ponytail, smoothing it out.

"Don't worry, I'm staying here, it's okay, go ahead. I'll use the time to do some work," she told him not too convincingly.

"Maybe you would have enjoyed being with Jelena at the spa more?" he asked her sweetly.

"And miss the chance to sit in a recording room for three hours, waiting around bored with no chance to go out for a ride, since the roads are full of crazy drivers? Oh, no, no, I'm stoic, Nucci, you don't know me, but I'm stoic."

"My Ranieri." He stroked her cheek. "Anyway, if you want, you can come over there to the control room so you can listen to me."

"Nucci, I have no ear for music."

He leaned over and whispered to her, sending a chill down her spine, "Well then, let me educate you in music in the coming days, Virginia."

A half-smile broke out on her face and she jumped back, turning on her phone. She opened her chat and laughed in delight as she read the various notifications. The allusion to the instrument was the most popular.

She texted: 'I can neither confirm nor deny, of course.' ;-)

She hesitated, but finally wrote on the keyboard: 'It's not that I'm in love, but... almost. But I'm afraid I'm just the next woman on the Maestro's interminable list of conquests.... What should I do? Do I give up or do I go ahead and get my heart broken?'

The friends responded in unison.

GO FOR IT!

Sara added: 'at least you will have something to tell your grandsons!!!'

She left her friends to their conjectures about her future and, having no desire to look at the emails received from SiVery Event, she shyly opened the door to the control room. The music of the cello struck her immediately, as if it had been behind the door waiting for her. On the opposite side of the glass Guglielmo, while playing, appeared in ecstasy, enraptured by the notes, taken away to a dimension that did not belong to her. He wondered what he was obstinately looking for in a woman to the point of changing one every month. What were the real motivations? And why had he and the Brazilian virago broken up?

The cellist raised his head and saw her. He smiled, with that expression on his mouth that Virginia loved. he pursed his lips and made a half smile, which made him even more charming.

Let's see where you take me, Maestro.

When the rehearsal was over, Guglielmo with a happy expression joined her and said, "It's time to go to the desert!"

They returned to the hotel and after changing, waited for the Range Rover that would take them to their destination, in the lobby of the Bulgari. They sat in a corner, facing the exit, cell phones in hand. Guglielmo was chatting with someone and sighing. He didn't look happy.

"Oh, no..." murmured Virginia as she saw Adriana enter. The virago greeted Guglielmo with a nod and exclaimed, "Olá, preciso de si; com António definimos as modalidades dos concertos."

He stood up and in a gentle tone said to her, "Forgive me, I guess she has to tell me something about the concert..."

The Brazilian Miss Universe began the conversation with a certain emphasis, though Guglielmo seemed more bored than anything else.

Jealousy wasn't a feeling she'd experienced in the past, however, that woman put her on edge, because objectively she was more beautiful and more attractive than her. And more ex. And more polyglot. And who knows what else.

Luckily for her, the concierge came to her rescue.

"Excuse me, Maestro, your car has arrived."

Guglielmo responded with a nod and quickly

dismissed Adriana. Then he took Virginia by the hand and said, "Ranieri, get ready for a thousand and one Arabian nights."

They climbed into the Range Rover and began the royal desert safari at the Dubai Reserve. From time to time the driver would stop the car pointing out and they could admire the camels and the gazelles.

"Absolutely marvelous," she murmured, gazing out at the golden desert and the magnificent dunes that stretched into the horizon, broken only by the vivid blue of the sky. Absent-mindedly, she pondered, "Pantone number 1118?" to pinpoint the exact hue of the sand.

"What's with these murmured numbers?" Guglielmo asked, curious.

Virginia shot him a playful glance. "Can't just hand out my secrets for free, can I? What level of intimacy have we reached, Nucci?"

His response caught her off guard. "Well, after everything we shared over Christmas, I would think we have gotten pretty close, wouldn't you agree?"

"I'm not entirely sure, Nucci. Let's see what tricks you have up your sleeve next, and then I might consider revealing my numbers..." She flashed a mischievous smile and took his hand.

Guglielmo clicked his tongue. "Did I ever mention that you're the most mysterious, enchanting, and bewitching woman I've ever met?"

"Nucci, with all the music you create, I expected a bit more creativity," she teased. "But don't assume that a few adjectives will unlock the combination to my heart," she added, laughing.

They finally arrived at the oasis where they would have had dinner. The round pond was set in the middle of the desert like a sapphire. Virginia couldn't help but emphatically state, "It's one sight after another..."

She watched as the last rays of sunlight faded into the dunes and the lights magically lit the waters of the reserve, surrounded by palm trees and dunes. The flames of the braziers twirled in the wind illuminating the table where they would dine.

The waiter brought the menu, shiny black, just like Virginia's dress. That day her pashmina was green. She adjusted it better, because the desert air had become a little more pungent than before.

"Ah, I'll have the smoked salmon and caviar with the grilled eggplant and the spiced lentil soup. Then, I'll have the seared cauliflower steak..." she said.

"I'll have the same, thank you," Guglielmo told the waiter, while handing over the menu.

Then taking her hand, he said:

"Tonight, I'd like to play just for you, Virginia. To make you feel what I feel."

Virginia looked at him and thought back at the

words of Adriana: *The next step will be the serenade, just for you. You, him, and his instrument. Oh my God! The virago was actually right! We're already at level 2 in his courting strategy.*

"And what will you play, Maestro?" she asked.

"I don't want to ruin the surprise."

Virginia said nothing. She rested her arm on the table and held her chin with her hand. She wiggled in her chair as she smiled at him and at one point raised her arm toward the waiter.

"Excuse me, I need an envelope and paper, please."

"What do you want to do?" Guglielmo was curious.

She smiled at him without answering. Once she had obtained the means she had asked for she said, "Close your eyes, Nucci." She scribbled something and closed the envelope. "Here. My guess as to what you will be playing this evening. If I'm right, only you will know, because you can always tell me a lie, but it's enough for me that your soul knows the truth."

Guglielmo shook his head and took the envelope, placing it in the inside pocket of his jacket and said nothing as the waiters arrived with the courses.

Virginia then changed the subject. She wanted

to take the opportunity to get to know the cellist better.

"So, how many concerts do you do a year?"

"On average, about a hundred. It depends."

"Heck, you're always on tour... And when's your birthday? Just asking. The internet is a little vague on this point. If I can know the truth, of course..."

Guglielmo frowned in response. "The twenty-fifth of June."

Virginia took a bite of the salmon and nodded. "Ah, sure, sure, because of St. William..."

"Mmm, you're prepared, Ranieri."

"And how old will you be next year?"

"Thirty-eight."

"Oh!" Virginia looked at him with a bewildered expression, and Guglielmo reacted, placing his fork on the napkin and coughing. That exclamation had made him uncomfortable. "Do you think I'm old?" He asked her.

Virginia passed her fork over her lips, mischievously. "I'm twenty-nine and I'm going to be thirty next year, on the twelfth of May... Do you think I'm old?"

"No, not at all!" he replied promptly.

She smiled at him.

Guglielmo suddenly stood up and took her hand, inviting her to get up as well. "Come, Ranieri, sit here," he pointed to the small sofa, "I really want to play for you, this way I'll find out if you were really able to read my mind, I'm eager to know..."

She stood up and, slowly holding up her arm and forcing Guglielmo to do the same, she moved lightly on the sand and sensually slipped off her pumps. Right foot, look at Guglielmo. Left foot, look at Guglielmo. She barely stirred the sand, sat down and smiled. "Then go ahead and play Maestro."

"It is a sonata by Beethoven. Number three." He lowered his eyes, sighed, and changed his expression. The bow and fingers pressed on the strings. And Beethoven's sonata stirred the desert air.

Magic.

The notes filled their souls, creeping into the innermost recesses of memory, bringing to light images that could belong to the past or to the future without the will interfering. The two spirits were rising.

At one point, midway through the performance, Virginia rose for real. Guglielmo watched her, with a certain attitude, continuing to play undaunted. And this was what she had hoped for: that he would continue to play.

She took a couple of steps, cautious, and saw that he put more strength into vibrating the strings and their glances, now intertwined, had engaged in a serious battle. Guglielmo let his irritation show, rippling his mouth not in the usual sensual way, but biting his lower lip even as he continued the performance. It was then that Virginia, in a sudden move, grabbed the cello's fingerboard with one hand and with the other the arm with which Guglielmo held the bow, suddenly stopping the music.

"Virginia!" he exclaimed angrily, but she in the sweetest tone she could muster answered him, "Listen to the silence, Maestro...hear the sand crunch under your bare feet, listen to the sound of stillness. Enjoy the silence."

His eyes had gone dark and they remained in that unnatural position for a long time, with neither of them deciding to move. The light breeze ruffled the cellist's forelock and Virginia let go, trying to fix it.

"Not here," he told her coldly and stood up, setting the cello down. He looked confused, agitated. He touched his hair and hovered near Virginia as if he wanted to do or say something without having the courage.

The waiter came back as Virginia put her shoes back on, returning to her seat.

"Would you like some dessert?" he asked them innocently.

CHAPTER 11.

The following days were quite intense due to the fact that the Four Bows had decided to rehearse both in the morning and in the afternoon, this because there were three concerts scheduled in Dubai, including that of New Year's Eve, but also and above all because, once back in Milan, they had a full program for the whole month of January. The Orchestra of the Teatro alla Scala had confirmed the dates from the seventh onwards. The fact that they were together on those days gave them the opportunity to rehearse what they had established for the Milanese schedule.

In the meantime, a delightful routine had been established between Guglielmo and Virginia. Breakfast in the room, often eaten several times, and light talk, like the sheets on which their bodies rested. After that Virginia would accompany him to morning rehearsals and at lunchtime they would go to one of the nearby shopping malls, until Guglielmo had to start playing again. In the evening they would have dinner either, alone or, together with the other Bows, having much fun.

The first two concerts had been held on the evenings of the 29th and 30th as a very exclusive event, and Virginia had not been invited. "I'm sorry that, for privacy reasons, I can't take you with me. Jelena can't come either, go figure... But to the Burj Khalifa concert, yes!" He said apologetically, but she didn't mind being alone those evenings and waiting for his return, late at night, falling asleep late with him.

That was why on the morning of December 31st, they were still in bed, him leaning against the headboard and her lying limply in his arms. They both absent-mindedly scrolled their fingers over their cell phones.

At one point, Virginia became more engaged by pressing fast, because she was responding to Filippo who was asking her about her current partner. On the other hand, some gossip magazine had relaunched a photo of Guglielmo together with her, during the welcome reception in Dubai, and Sara had promptly circulated the photo on their chat.

"Who is the guy you're chatting with?" asked Guglielmo. He tightened his arm more around Virginia's waist and she moved the display to hide it from his view. She answered vaguely, "A friend..."

"A friend." He repeated, not concealing his displeasure and taking her cell phone.

"Hey! Give it back!"

"Here, here...what kind of friend?"

"Jealous?" She rubbed her back against him.

"Did you sleep with him?"

Virginia turned to look at him mischievously, but couldn't bring herself to tell a lie. "Um, no just a little kiss... Do you know that thanks to him, I came very close to entering your world when I was seventeen?"

"Oh, really? With what instrument? His?"

Languid eye: "No, no... No... Filippo and I are part of this group of friends. From way back. You know those people you can always confide in? The ones you can call if you're sick and they don't ask you anything, but they take you around to do stupid things and only later, if you're ready, do you tell them what's wrong? The ones I call the trust-friends?"

"No, I don't."

"Jeez Nucci, don't you have any real friends? What about your brothers? What about the other three Bows?"

"Mmm," he said, adjusting himself better and clinging to her. "Let me think, then, according to what you said, definitely my brother Giorgio. Okay, as you say, let's include my sister too. And Cori, I think. And you, of course."

"Oh don't even think about putting me on your list, Nucci. A guy like you is capable of calling at three in the morning just to say the woman on duty isn't what he expected."

"Hey, I'm not like that!"

"Of course you are! Why, it's a miracle you still remember my name. And turn off the instrument," she patted him on the thigh. "It's always on for God's sake!"

He chuckled as he tickled her. "Stop it!" They laughed. Virginia grabbed his arms and stopped him. "Now it's my turn, to tell a brief nostalgic memory by fishing it out of my past. So. Filippo, with whom I had the world's shortest relationship..."

"Who left who?"

"It was by mutual agreement."

"And you still stayed friends afterwards? As in close friends?"

"Shut up, Nucci, and listen to me!" she said in a mocking way. "Filippo at one point had decided to form a band. My friends Sara and Monica, would be the backing singers, Davide piano, Filippo and Gabriele, guitar and bass respectively, while Massimo," she mischievously touched the muscles in his arms, "would play the drums."

"Well, as you can see, you don't need a drum set to develop certain muscles... In addition to texting, are you also seeing this Fillipo guy?"

"So Filippo," she answered him as she continued, amused by the question she decided not to answer, "decided that I was going to be the frontwoman!"

"I believe you, you always put the hottest chick in front of the band, music marketing 101."

Virginia looked at him and blushed, "Oh, well, thank you..."

"So going back to this... Filippo," the cellist pressed on, "have you tried to get back better again? Has he made a move again?"

"No, we're just friends, I told you. Too bad, what with school and all, we disbanded the group after not even a year. On the other hand, the friendship remained very strong."

"Even a tad too much for my taste, here give it here..." Guglielmo reached out again and took her cell phone. "Let me see this guy."

"Give me my phone back you brute!" she said, teasing him.

"No way, I have the sanctimonious right to know who is chatting with my woman..." Guglielmo replied ironically as he read the contact's name, "Filippo Patruno..."

"Hey!" complained Virginia again, "For privacy reasons, you absolutely can't! Give it back!" she intimated, but despite her protests, Guglielmo held the phone and turned on his stomach, fiddling with the keyboard. Virginia climbed on his back desperately trying to get the phone back. "Give it to me!"

"Wait, wait, I want to do something..." he laughed bluntly. "I'm done, I'm done." The music started. The phone started playing *Ti amo*, by Umberto Tozzi.

Virginia clapped her hand to her face. "My God you really are old, Maestro! This song goes way back before I was even born!"

"It's one of my favorites and besides, it describes exactly how I feel right now, *ti amo*, I love you."

"Aw, that's sweet," she said.

"You know what I like about you Ranieri?"

"Let's hear it Nucci."

"It's the fact that I don't fully understand you." He clicked his tongue. "I don't know, you're different from the others. You have that aloof attitude towards me, you allow yourself to interrupt me while I'm playing, you chat with another man while you're in my arms, you tease me... All of this on one hand makes me angry and on the other hand makes me want you more and more. I want your body, but I also want your soul...".

Despite all the sensible warnings echoing in her mind, Virginia had to admit that, bit by bit, the Maestro was claiming more of her heart with each passing day.

CHAPTER 12.

At nine o'clock in the evening they went to the Burj Khalifa, the tallest skyscraper in the world.

They arrived at the observation deck called At the Top Sky and Virginia agreed on the choice of name. Very appropriate. According to her, it could have been called "Beyond the Sky", because the view was breathtaking, amplified by the scenographic effect of the large windows that circled all around, sparkling because of the metal inserts, and reflecting the lights of the skyline and the interior. You could see Dubai as if you were flying over it or jumping with a parachute.

"Impressive..." she said, scratching near her ear. Someone too close to the windows got dizzy from the vertigo, and Virginia took advantage of that distraction to let the pressure out of her ears..

"Virginia, what are you doing?" asked Guglielmo, tugging slowly. She gave him a nod, waited a moment, and returned to normal. "My ears were plugged, the elevator went up so fast it caused me to take off."

Guglielmo gave her an expression of

disapproval.

"Jeez, sorry, dad." she said sarcastically.

Although he hadn't concealed his nervousness, Guglielmo hadn't let go of her hand and after a short while, in a tone that appeared gentle but betrayed a certain impatience, he told her, "Go stand next to Jelena. And be good."

Oh, my goodness, Maestro. How agitated we are.

The chairs had been arranged to surround a small stage that had its back to the stained glass windows where the Four Bows would be performing. Guglielmo joined them and Virginia greeted Cori's wife cheerfully. "Hi Jelena, how are you?"

"I'm well thank you dear. Hopefully the trip will be over quickly. I don't know if it's the same for Guglielmo, but Cori is restless. In fact, to be honest, he's really unbearable!"

"Eh, let's just say that being near Guglielmo these days has been a bit of a roller coaster ride , and consider that mine, as I imagine yours, is in no way meant to be an insult to them."

"Ha, ha, ha..." Jelena laughed and paused to look at Virginia. She sat up better and turned slightly toward her, as if seeing her for the first time. "Have you known him long?"

The question was both unexpected and expected. Jelena had that sort of look that seemed almost maternal, softened by her round face and a glance that, despite its chilly edge, found some warmth in the golden curls framing her features.

"No," Virginia answered truthfully, "we've been together for a week and it's been quite a whirlwind. One moment we were on a flight to Vienna, just before Christmas, and now here we are, eight hundred feet above the desert. Hope I don't end up falling!" she laughed nervously.

"You'll be fine. Guglielmo is a strange soul. Cori has known him since they were twenty-five, twenty-six years old, but he has never been able to pin him down. Still, I can see that you're a smart girl, unlike..."

Jelena dropped the sentence for a moment and Virginia thought: *Unlike who?*

"Let's just say you're different. Don't let him crush you with his personality."

Who,   me?   Miss do-whatever-you-want-with-me after just twenty-five seconds of talking to him on a plane? Some smart girl that I am...

The virago meanwhile had made her way to the center of the room. The long, black evening gown with satin sleeves made her appear even taller. And slender. And the silver earrings and necklace made her look even more beautiful. All the men followed her words in religious silence; some, Virginia noticed, even with their mouths clearly open, and not for a yawn that did not come to fruition.

Adriana took the microphone and in perfect English introduced the Four Bows: Coriolan Kovács, Tamas Nemeth, János Horvat and Guglielmo Nucci. Viola, violin, violin, cello. Brief presentation of the first three strings. Hungarian, studies at the Liszt Music Academy in Budapest, beginning of their careers in Italy and finally the meeting with Guglielmo. With him, Adriana lingered a little longer. She stood at his side, a hand blandly on his shoulder. It didn't bother Virginia, not too much, but in her heart she rejoiced when Guglielmo bent down to fix the cuff of his pants, in fact, elegantly eliminating contact.

"Perhaps not many of you know how Maestro Nucci became a cellist, but today, I want to share with you his secret." The virago knew how to hold the stage, you had to give her credit for that, and as she sensuously spoke those words, she walked towards her and Jelena.

"Guglielmo was very small and his grandmother Vittoria, a famous violinist who also played at La Scala in Milan..."

Oh, no, please, please, please... Don't say he was five years old and staying with his siblings....

"She decided it was time for Guglielmo to learn how to play a bow. But which one? "

Well Maestro, whatever happened to the thing that only a few of us knew the truth about your beginnings? Adriana-Virago one, Ranieri zero.

"It wasn't easy, having such a young child choose an instrument to play, so his grandmother took him to a concert by the best cellist in the world, Maestro Mstislav Leopoldovich Rostropovich. And since then, Guglielmo hasn't stopped playing the cello!"

You mean to tell me that Adriana really doesn't know the real story? What happened?! That's one point for Ranieri who scores! Italy one, Brazil zero!

She was secretly rejoicing when Jelena turned towards her, this time with an arctic gaze. She gave her a courteous smile of circumstance and involuntarily raised her face to see Guglielmo, who was staring at her. He nodded at her and smiled. Guglielmo then stood up and asked for the microphone and the virago went towards him with resolute steps and handed over the device with a fake smile.

"Thank you all," Guglielmo began to say, "And thank you in particular to our gracious host who allows us to play in the most evocative location in the world. Again, thank you on behalf of the Four Bows." He then looked at Virginia. Despite the audience, he seemed to have eyes only for her. "If you'll allow me,

I'd like to start with a sonata. It is probably little known and is not in our usual repertoire, but I would like to dedicate it to a person who is very special to me and who made me appreciate it again. Virginia, thank you." He bowed in her direction as his lips pursed sensuously.

Aw, Nucci.

"We will offer a revisiting of Giovanni Gabrieli's Sonata Number Twenty-one for three violins. Coriolan Kovács will demonstrate that he is a fine violinist as well as an excellent violist. After that we will move on to our usual performances. Enjoy!"

Virginia had never heard that sonata before. The Dubai skyline had turned into a rich, golden hue. She shut her eyes and tilted her head back, letting a tide of memories wash over her. Suddenly, she felt as though she was twelve again, standing in the heart of a decadent yet magnificent church with towering walls that seemed to reach into the heavens. Back then, she'd stood with her head held high, spinning, determined to make those walls reverberate and send a musical message to the heavens. It was in that moment that she realized the music she had been seeking all this time was the very one playing now.

CHAPTER 13.

The day after the concert, Guglielmo was still asleep when Virginia, around ten o'clock, opened her eyes. She tried to be quiet, but he turned around. "Where are you going?"

"You've got your radar up all the time, Nucci... I'm hungry, I'm going down to breakfast and then I was thinking of going to the spa. You can join me there if you'd like."

"Mmm, if you wait a bit, I'll come too..." He tried to grab her, but she slipped out, "But I'm hungry..." she whined.

"All right, Ranieri, I'll come find you later, wherever you are." He gave her an auspicious touch.

Thank you...

She took only her Chanel bag, her life companion, because by now she was used to putting only the essentials, including credit card and cell phone, and off to the restaurant Il Café where she treated herself to the Roma menu. Cappuccino, freshly squeezed orange juice, basket of fresh pastries, as well as butter and jam that were of the highest quality.

The cream on top of the cap had Bulgari writing made with cocoa, and the tartlet with berries looked like a little gem that, instead of raspberries, appeared to have been decorated with rubies sprinkled with powdered sugar.

Oh God, this is heaven, she thought.

After the ecstasy of breakfast, she went to the spa. She was going to relax in one of the bayfront loungers, but in the locker room, she had a nasty surprise. Her period had come.

Oh no! Heck, with all this tourbillon of excitement, it slipped my mind that it was due today...bummer! Lucky for me, I have the tampax in the room.

She walked quickly toward the suite, but slowed her pace as she heard noises coming from inside. Laughter to be precise.

She leaned her hands against the doorframe to listen better.

She hesitated.

Nucci, seriously? We haven't even gotten to level two and you're already....

She slowly opened the door. She introduced only her head and peered, narrowing her eyes because she wasn't wearing her glasses. The sofas, the small table, the glass window, the pool. At the edge of the pool was a woman. Tall, thin, shiny black hair, straight. Loose on her shoulders.

She closed the door and slowly rummaged through her purse. Her hands were trembling, her eyes were already flooded with tears, which, no matter how hard she tried, she could not hold back. She put on her glasses and opened the door wide, opening it wider than before, but being careful not to make noise and not to be discovered. Despite her fogged vision, she saw that on the opposite side of the pool, closer to the entrance of the room, there was another woman, also tall, long and curly hair of a color she couldn't define because of the desert sunlight.

Not one but two women?

Guglielmo arrived, glasses in hand. He was dressed in a t-shirt and shorts. She heard him say, "How nice that you are already here! Today the fun begins!"

The woman with long black hair, in that instant dived into the pool, while the curly-haired woman, taking the glass, reached out and put a hand on Guglielmo's shoulder. "I'm so happy too!"

The woman stood up on her toes and kissed Guglielmo lightly on the cheek.

Virginia pulled over, because she didn't want to see more than she had already seen. She stared at the door. Fade out. End of story.

By fun, you mean an orgy Maestro? Well, I'm sorry but I'm not into that!

143

She was angry, disappointed, furious with him, with herself, with the world. The tears were falling inexorably, huge drops that ended up on her hands, on her arms. She changed her glasses, took her sunglasses and headed for the lobby.

She glanced at the virago on one of the sofas, her luggage beside her.

Ah, I thought it was her, maybe she'll catch up with them later.

Adriana came over and started talking. The tone was provoking.

"Going shopping dear? All alone? Without him?"

Virginia said nothing to her and spoke to the concierge. "I need a cab, please."

The virago didn't seem intent on giving up and continued as if nothing was wrong.

"Last night, did you hear the little story about how the Maestro approached the cello? I surprised you, didn't I? He tells the same story to everyone. Let me repeat my advice to you, enjoy these days with him while you can, but if I were you, I would already start thinking about your future without him."

"What, are you also in charge of getting him new ones?" Virginia's eyes flamed and the virago looked at her in surprise. A man called out to her, "Adriana!"

At that point she touched her shoulder and

gave her an evil smile as he walked away. "Have fun while you can, dear."

She remained staring at the swaying back of the Brazilian woman, until the concierge said, "Your cab will be here shortly, Miss Ranieri."

"Thank you. Can you add that to Mr. Nucci's bill?"

"Of course, Miss Ranieri."

At least the ride to the airport, a##&^le!

On the way to the airport she was thinking about how to book her flight. It was a little difficult from the phone or maybe it was just that she didn't have the energy.

She called Claudio, her colleague.

"Hi. I have a favor to ask you, big as a house, and I can't explain it."

"Well good morning to you too Virginia, are you still in Dubai with the Maestro?"

"Claudio, I can't answer your questions."

"Fine, what do you need from me?"

"Can you book me a flight from Dubai, destination Milan? I don't care about the cost, I want to leave as soon as possible. I'll call Carolina right now and let her know. I'll adjust with her when I get back to the office." A sob escaped her.

"Virginia don't worry, I'll tell Carolina and set it up right away. I'll text you as soon as I get the ticket confirmation. Do you also want a car to take you home from the airport?"

She sighed, thinking that would probably be appropriate.

"Yes, thank you Claudio, you are truly a friend." She blew his nose. "I don't have any luggage. Just myself."

She arrived at the airport and, while waiting for the message from his colleague, went to the Marhaba Lounge. She needed a quiet place for her stormy soul.

She sat in one of the red chairs and waited. Her stomach was in turmoil, her head was throbbing, and she was holding the phone tightly in her hand. Her fingers were beginning to ache, too.

More than anything else, the twinges came from the heart. In pieces.

The phone vibrated.

[Whatsapp message from Nucci]
Where are you? I'm looking for you everywhere. Sorry I didn't get out of bed right away, but I needed a full recharge. I'm wide awake now!

She glanced at the screen and thought sourly: No wonder you're wide awake, double charging, right? a##&^le...

[Whatsapp message from Nucci]

I'm at The Lounge, sitting next to the Monica Vitti painting. Come on down. It's all for us.

Fleeting glance at the notification, with no message showing as read.

[Whatsapp message from Nucci]
??? Ranieri, where are you? Today we finally start the real vacation and I wanted to tell you something, I am impatient....

Virginia opened the chat, clicked on more options, her finger had a doubt, but then she forced herself to push. LOCK. And in an instant Guglielmo was gone from her life. She felt like throwing up and ran to the bathroom. She shut herself inside, crying in despair, always with the cell phone in her hand, waiting for Claudio to extract her from that desert.

CHAPTER 14.

She stayed on the sofa all through Epiphany day. Her tears had ceased, leaving her with a nose too sore to even contemplate blowing.

Her friends had arrived very early.

"I'm a rag. Why did you come? It's not like anything's gonna change..."

"Stop it, Virgi, what are you saying? We'll give you a hand. Let's clean the kitchen first. And tomorrow, you plan to go to the office?" asked Monica, looking at Virginia still in her pajamas.

Go ahead and say it. Do you plan to go to the office looking like that?

"At least I'm doing something..."

The two disappeared behind the door and Virginia heard them talking.

"I'm here and I'm not deaf..."

Sara looked out the pass-through window, which divided the two small rooms, and shyly murmured, "You know I follow him on Instagram..."

"Oh, no. Please don't. Don't start..."

"It looks like he's sick. Very sick. They've had to cancel their scheduled concerts here in Milan..."

"Sara... I couldn't care less..."

He's sick?? What about me then?

"I've read the comments," her friend continued, "They say it's because of the fact that the mystery woman, that's you, left him. Some also say that this woman, also you, was the one..."

Virginia didn't know whether to laugh, cry, or get angry. "First of all, the mystery woman isn't necessarily me."

"It's you. We call you that when we leave comments." Sara blushed at her choice of verbal persona.

Virginia rose from the couch and squinted, "Are you telling me that you," she pointed her finger at her, "You make comments about me, knowing who I am? And you call me a mystery woman?"

The friend did not respond, but was obviously embarrassed.

"Maybe," Monica chimed in, "You could call him and you could clear the air, no?"

She began with a quiet tone, and then increased it as she spoke, until she reached high notes, which even when she had tried to sing she had never been able to produce.

"Look, girls. I get it. He's good loking, all right? He's handsome. He's good at music, he's a god in bed. What do you want me to say? There, now you know. He's smart. He's funny. He's got them all, all right? But he's also a womanizer. I'd never been swept off my feet by the first guy that came along, but it happened. I'd probably do it again if I had to. With him, I mean. But I was wrong to trust him, to let go, to believe that I could be different. Unique. So what if he's hurting, I couldn't care less. I mean, can you imagine? *I'm* the one hurting, not him! You're supposed to be my friends!" she yelled, pounding her hand hard on her chest. "Guglielmo is the a##&^le and I'm the one who has to justify herself??"

She opened the door to let them leave. "I don't want to talk anymore. I'll get over it. And, Sara, do me a favor, write it in the chat that the mystery woman is also hurting! At least the prick gets to know how I feel too! What the heck!"

The next day she showed up at the office wearing sunglasses. She arrived early, hid herself behind her desk, and when Elisabetta arrived, she told her not to let anyone pass except for Siveri, just in case he showed up.

Obviously everyone in the company knew about the brief, albeit intense, affair between her and the Maestro and that it was over, but she was determined not to talk to anyone about it for at least a few weeks, waiting for the dust to settle.

At about ten-thirty, there was a light knock at the door and Elisabetta emerged, her red forelock in front of her eyes.

Virginia took off her glasses and stared at her annoyed. "What is it?" It hadn't even been an hour since she'd told her she didn't want to be bothered.

"Um, some flowers came... for you" she whispered.

"Throw them in the bin." She told her, imagining the sender.

What more does he want?!

"It's not that simple. The florist says he has more down and, well, I don't know where to put them anymore. Oh, and then there are some suitcases too." Elisabetta stood waiting for instructions and then she stood up, walked around the desk, leaning in front of it and nodded to her. "Alright, have everything brought in."

Elisabetta swung the door open wide ushering in the attendants. The first two men entered with suitcases and placed them at Virginia's feet. There were her two bags, plus two others, Louis Vuitton. She noticed that labels had been placed in all of them, with two large golden letters: VR. And underneath, first and last name imprinted in full. Soon, an army of florists followed, each carrying a box of delicate roses in varying shades of pink—some white, others peachy, but mostly pink. The room swiftly bloomed into a fragrant spectrum of colors.

"Virginia, I was told the baskets are 148..."

She was caught off guard and watched as the

men came in and placed those baskets everywhere. On the floor, on the two shelves, on the small armchair. A man asked her, "Ms. Ranieri?"

"Yes..."

"This is the first one," he told her. The basket of roses he was holding was larger than the others and the attendant walked over to the desk, trying to find a space between the laptop and the video.

"Ah, wait, I'll make room for you." She moved a few pens and notepads out of the way, and as the florist gently set it down, she saw the envelope peeking out. She opened it and started reading.

My beloved Queen,

When I think of you my soul soars to heaven. Like the day we were at the Burj Khalifa, on the 148th floor. Do you remember? Please call me. Guglielmo

Yes, Nucci it's been twenty days...not twenty years. Of course I remember.

She leaned over a basket that had been placed on the ground and opened another message.

My beloved Queen,

The course of true love has never run smoothly. Please give me a chance to explain. G.

And another.

My beloved Queen,

If music were the food of love, one would have to keep playing. But I can't anymore, not without you. I hope I still have a chance. Please call me. G.

The words were touching, she had to admit. That, please call me, was a poignant plea.

The parade continued for a good half hour. A few baskets had to be placed just outside the office door, and Virginia saw many of her colleagues huddled together, admiring that spectacle of flowers. A couple of women were talking and Virginia clearly heard one say that it was her fault.

Go figure...

Elisabetta, help me collect all the cards. After that, let's organize a van. I want the flowers to be taken to a non-profit association."

When they were finished, Virginia opened the last drawer of the desk and indicated to her assistant to leave the cards there. They fell from their hands, scattered and some rolled out.

"You know, Virginia," Elisabetta told her, picking one up and arranging the others better. "I know I'm not supposed to tell you anything, but I've never seen as many roses as I did today. And all these cards he wrote to you, well, he's definitely in love with you. Maybe you should give him a call."

Don't you usually talk about you and Elia? She thought.

Did you have to start making sense today of all days? Yes, I've never seen so many roses either. No one has ever given them to me before. Yes, the letters are all handwritten. But if he was really in love with me, why were those women there? No, never. I'll never call him again.

She locked the drawer without saying anything.

CHAPTER 15.

Virginia and Sara had a scheduled their usual rendezvous behind the Duomo, at Piazza dei Mercanti, at three in the afternoon. Their shopping excursion was just a cover for a specific mission—one they undertook every fourteenth of February without fail. Their destination? One of the renowned jewelers on Corso Vittorio Emanuele.

"Good morning," the clerk chimed in cheerfully.

"Good morning," Sara responded with a measured tone. "My friend here is getting married next September and would like to try on some engagement rings."

This annual routine hadn't been uncovered yet. Perhaps it was because the store was vast, and the staff changed frequently. Or perhaps no one paid much attention to the purpose of their visit, viewing them merely as potential customers.

The man ushered them to a set of plush, red velvet chairs, positioned before a small table adorned in the same soft fabric, where he planned to display the jewelry.

"Let's see, platinum is all the rage this year. We have this classic square cut, why don't you try it on..." He presented the sizable diamond ring for Virginia to test. She slipped it on, her expression a bit pained.

"My dear," Sara interjected, "it's the year of platinum..." Their gazes locked, and Virginia couldn't help but laugh mischievously.

Attempting to maintain composure, she hesitated, "I was just thinking...I'm not sure..." Her thoughts trailed off, leaving her at a loss for a witty reply. But before she could gather her words, the attendant intervened, "Would you prefer something with a gem other than a diamond? Perhaps this ruby..." He gestured to the adjacent ring, then added, "...or maybe this sapphire instead."

"It's beautiful..."

"The blue heart." The clerk gently wiped it with a cloth and handed it to her. "It's a ring embellished by the fact that the sapphire heart is surrounded by sixteen diamonds, all mounted on white gold."

She put it on and continued to gaze at the jewel, letting the sparkle of the diamonds and the blue of the stone captivate her. The color reminded her of the pond at the Dubai oasis where Guglielmo had tried to play for her that night. "It was so beautiful..."

"What was so beautiful?" Sara asked her.

Virginia's silence was eloquent and Sara with a frown, said turning to the clerk, "Well, then if you can leave us a little note of the type of ring..."

The man, after securing the jewels, including the blue heart that Virginia reluctantly returned, disappeared into the back, returning with a note.

"Here you go."

They walked out onto the porch and, unlike previous years when they laughed like crazy, Virginia sighed. Sara began to speak, understanding, "Virgi, you'll see that things will work out..."

Shee hugged her.

"This time it's going to take a little longer... Darn me and love at first sight..."

"I know. Besides, you broke up without explaining yourselves and-"

"Sara. Again?"

"Well, it's the truth, though, isn't it!"

"So if Massimo were to cheat on you, you would talk to him and try to understand."

"I would kill him first. But if he asked me, yes. I'd talk to him."

"Mmm, now why do I find it hard to believe. The truth is you wouldn't want to see him again."

"I'd argue with him first. I'd confront him. You didn't even do that. You walked away, without telling him to his face what you thought. That's why you're still hurting. More than for him, you should do it for yourself. Listen to Auntie Sara here."

"All right, *Auntie Sara*, I'll think about it."
Then, trying to change the subject, she asked. "And
what about you? Where is Massimo taking you
tonight?"

Sara and Massimo were the only couple that
had formed within their friends group. They were
predestined, the others knew it and no one had
interfered, preserving that tender love blossomed
between the school desks and continued to evolve
over time. They had already been living together for a
couple of years, but they weren't talking about
marriage yet.

"He said there's a place near the columns of
San Lorenzo that he wants us to try. A typical
trattoria, red and white checkered tablecloths and all,
kind of like the cartoon Lilli and the Tramp..." she
said laughing.

"Well, at least you get to go out with your
beau. Me, I'll just sit back and watch the usual black
and white romance movie crying and feeling
miserable, thinking that everyone is engaged and
living happily ever after except me..."

"Not everyone. Filippo broke up with Adele."

"Oh, no, when?"

"He wrote it in the chat last night..."

"But no, they must have had an argument; she
wrote that Adele left him stranded..."

"Yes, but not in the sense that she took the car...in the sense that she left him."

Virginia stopped and picked up her cell phone. She read the last few messages and stared at Sara. "Oh, poor thing. I read the text hastily. I even told him to go green and take the bicycle… I made the usual fool of myself uh?"

"He texted me separately and told me you made him laugh. You are our usual Virginia..."

"Wait, let me text him." She typed quickly as she inquired further. "Was it her that wanted to break up?"

"Yes, it seems she is already seeing someone else..."

"Nooo! Oh my God, Fili..."

"You know, you two should be together," Sara told her.

"Sara, please don't start with that again. It's not that because we've both been cheated on, then we should get together. Two wrongs don't make a right. The answer is always no. N.O. We're not right for each other."

"All right, all right. I suggested the idea to Filippo too and he said the same thing..."

"Oh you are a horrible human being," Virginia said mockingly. "The body isn't cold yet and you're already formulating new love strategies..." She laughed. "Okay, I will confess that we dated in high school for a little while"

At that revelation, Sara raised her eyebrow. "Ah..."

"So now that I tell you we tried, you're still not happy?" Virginia giggled. "Anyway, it seemed like it might work and instead we kissed and it felt like I was kissing my brother... Weird feeling, really... And I don't even have a brother!"

"What about him?"

"Ditto. The fact that we are friends, however, allowed us to move on with no regrets. We looked at each other and said it was okay. Are you happy now, Auntie Sara?"

"And you never thought about it again?"

"Jeez, you're making such a big deal of this thing. If it doesn't work, it doesn't work..."

"Okay, good. Look, if you want, I'll text Massimo and stay home with you and cry in front of the TV. "

"Are you crazy? Go to your man. Besides, I have an appointment at seven."

"Oh, but then you could have told me before, couldn't you!" exclaimed Sara. "And who is this?"

"Don't get excited. It's with a realtor, about an apartment..."

By now she had decided to put down roots in Milan and buying a house had become a priority. Even if, lately, scrolling through all those ads, she had to admit that the thought of going it alone was a bit heavy. Every now and then, she lingered on the two-storey houses in the suburbs, a small garden full of flowers, a few scattered toys that suggested the presence of children. However, they were fleeting moments of a life she didn't have.

The one-bedroom apartment she was going to see that evening, from the photos, didn't seem too bad. Plus it was close to the office and the price seemed fair. It wasn't until she got together with the realtor that she realized she knew nothing about the art of being a salesperson.

Virginia was standing in the middle of the room trying to remember the pictures, which didn't look remotely like what the woman was proposing to her.

"So, this is perfect for you, an up and coming professional. In this corner, you can set up your kitchen, while here," she said pointing to the opposite corner "...you can have a small bathrooml. The living room and the bedroom would be there and here."

Virginia looked at the small square room where the realtor had created a non existent flat. To her it seemed more like an enlarged shoebox.

The cell phone rang, distracting her from the disappointment.

"One moment, excuse me," she said to the real estate agent.

"Martina, hi. I can't talk right now, can I call you back?"

Martina replied agitatedly, "Virginia, Siveri asked for you. It's urgent! He's waiting for you."

Shee closed the call. "Forgive me, but I have an emergency. Let me think about it and I'll let you know tomorrow if I'm interested."

Of course she was going to tell her no, but she didn't want to waste time, in case that saleswoman got it into her head to try to convince her otherwise; she wasn't wrong because she left her by saying, "Make up your mind quickly, you don't want to lose this little gem of a flat!"

She nearly puffed in her face before leaving that dump and still on the stairs of the apartment building, she called her boss directly.

"Good evening Mister Siveri, I was told you were looking for me?"

"Aren't you in the office?"

Virginia rolled her eyes. "I had a personal appointment, but I'm close by, I'm on my way back."

"That's fine, because I'd rather talk in person. I'll be at the office until around 8:30. Afterwards, my wife has a dinner party planned - I can't miss it. Do you think you can get her before then?"

She looked at her watch. Quarter to eight. "Yes, absolutely." She answered and began to run, despite her heels. She hoped she wouldn't fall.

When she arrived at the office, she fixed her hair and took a deep breath before knocking at Siveri's door.

"Come in!" she heard.

Once, she entered, her boss looked at his watch.

"Eight minus five. Did you run?" He asked her rhetorically, motioning for her to sit down. She tried to pull herself together, swallowing.

"Water?"

"No, thank you."

"Do you know that I never got a chance to ask you again how you came up with the idea of buying those ties?"

It had the air of a rebuke. After three months, Virginia no longer expected to have to justify herself for that acid green napkin incident. Evidently she was wrong. He had made her go to the office, at that hour, just to talk about that.

"I know, it was all my fault, I take full responsibility."

She remained still, standing with her hands behind her back. She was used to talking to men like that, because her father was one of them and she knew that making excuses would only make the situation worse. And she wanted to resolve the matter quickly.

"Ha, ha, ha...I wish I could have been there,

that must have been a lot of fun..." chuckled the boss. "And tell me, Virginia, what was the accessory you chose for the women?"

"A corsage, with a yellow daffodil."

"Ah, sure, very apt, bravo..." Siveri smiled.

What's this all about? She thought.

"Look, I'll get right to the point. We have a one and a half, two million project coming up. In the sense that the client is giving us a budget of up to two, but with the indication that if we can still be maintain it to one point five, he would appreciate it."

"Right..." Virginia still didn't understand.

"The client is Marquis Manfredi Pietro Maria Casarinucci de' Tomei."

"Ah! Any other name?" she exclaimed laughing, but Siveri did not laugh. "I'm sorry, but these noblemen, who like to be called still with all these names... do they know it's 2023?" By now she had recovered all her breath.

Darn it Virgi! When will you ever learn to keep your mouth quiet!

"The Marquis is a friend of the CEO of the football team you were in charge of, and it seems that he spoke highly of us, and particularly of you, so de' Tomei decided to approach our company. He is the son of the perhaps better known Arturo Leone Maria." He explained the boss, in a low voice, as if that information might be enlightening to Virginia.

"Er... should I know him?"

"He was kidnapped in the 70's and released after a few months. A bad page in the news."

Virginia shook her head again.

"Of course, you are too young, how could you know? Doesn't matter. Anyway, the son, Manfredi, has basically asked me to organize a trip of two, maximum three days, starting next Sunday. A small group of friends will participate, and we will have to take care of food, lodging and above all entertainment. The Marquis wants to celebrate his fiancee by giving her an unusual setting for her birthday. A short, but intense trip out of town."

"Nice. And when's her birthday?"

"Tuesday. And he told me that he would like to stay in Italy. In addition, there are two firm points: that you, Virginia, will coordinate the event and that, to cheer the evenings of the guests, we will have to absolutely use the group of the Four Bows...."

Siveri left the sentence mid-air, and Virginia reacted bluntly.

"You're kidding, right?"

"I'm afraid not. The Marquis has been categorical and will send an email with the details the moment we confirm that we will accept on his terms. And besides all this, the problem is that today is Monday and the departure date is set for this Sunday. Are you up for it?"

"But, I mean, how can we even know the Four Bows would be up for it, they would surely-"

"They've already agreed," Siveri said interrupting her.

She looked at her boss. He certainly would not take no for an answer. She was going to have to work with Guglielmo and that was the last thing she wanted. Seeing that scoundrel again was not on her agenda. Her head was spinning. Who knows why Adriana came to mind. The virago. The revenge.

"Fine." She muttered more to herself than to Siveri.

"Thank you Virginia; I'll confirm by email right away, so we can buy time. We will need to uh, contact the Four Bows, but I can do that if you want. The de' Tomei said that the Maestro has asked to know where they're going to play, for issues of musician placement, acoustics, things like that."

There was a moment of Silence. It was late, she wanted to go home. And for nothing in the world she would have wanted to call Nucci. But then again, this was her job. And no one could tell her how to do her job.

"I'll call him." She finally said.

She went back to her desk and dialed Guglielmo's number: even though she had deleted it from her phone she still knew it by heart.

The phone rang several times, but no one

answered.

"Hello?"

That deep familiar voice.

"Hi."

Virginia took a moment before continuing to speak. The words had to come out firm and she succeeded, "Guglielmo, I think you know why I'm calling you. I just want to know if you have any problems working with me."

"How about you?"

"I don't have any problems. It's a job, like any other."

"Good, I have no problems either. However, it would be better if we talked face to face. Before I embark on this field trip with you, I want some guaranteed."

He needs guarantees... the prick...

"Fine." She answered him without emphasis and Guglielmo said coldly, "Meet me for lunch. I'll call you tomorrow."

When the call ended, Virginia resumed breathing. She touched her belly, because a strange feeling had pervaded her. Instinct urged her to go back to Siveri and cancel everything. Her soul, however, begged her to see him one last time.

CHAPTER 16.

The clock read eleven o'clock and Virginia was pacing the room with the pen in hand, as if it were a sword, talking to herself. "Perhaps I might consider Lake Como or-"

She gasped when Elisabetta walked into the office, saying, "Sorry Virginia it's just that you don't take calls, but this one seems urgent. One of the Four Bows says he needs to talk to you."

"Oh, yeah, put him on."

"Virginia," Guglielmo said, "I made reservations at Cicci and Saporiti. Do you know where that is?"

"Yes."

"Let's meet in an hour so we don't catch the lunch break mess." His voice was resolute.

And sexy.

She stayed with the handset in her hand, rocked back in her chair for a few minutes, and decided she wasn't going to stay in the office and wait.

"I'm out to lunch and don't want to be disturbed," she told Elisabetta and went downstairs, taking her laptop with her.

The place was a small trattoria, the food was quite good and it wasn't pretentious, although, when she entered, a waiter came up to her.

"Hi, there should be a table reserved under the name Nucci."

The Maestro wasn't there yet so she pulled out her laptop. She had already started to think about the trip and was nervous because she had very little time. The budget would allow her to act quickly, but without ideas she could do little. And it was already Tuesday. She sent an email to Claudio and Martina with an eloquent subject: any suggestions?

Suddenly, a jingle made her raise her head. It was Guglielmo. He was leaning, in a corner of the table, his keys, his cell phone, his sunglasses, and he was moving, as if he was occupying his territory. The voice, somber, accompanied those gestures, "Is there a place where you don't work?"

Virginia responded stymied. "We're not here to talk about me."

The cellist took the chair, sank into it and shook his head, "Okay, then let's talk about us. Did you get the roses?"

"Don't start."

"So you did get them." He opened the menu and continued talking behind it. "A fan of mine a few weeks ago wrote on Instagram that the mystery woman is still suffering."

"I don't have social profiles, I don't follow this kind of news." She thought back to the day when, still in Dubai, she took herself off everything: deleted every profile possible and unimaginable. To avoid him contacting her. To avoid those eyes. And now she had them in front of her. She lowered her gaze and sighed.

"That makes two of us. However, Jelena runs the Four Bows page. And she told me this. The fan says she knows the mystery woman well. So I replied to her privately. And I asked her if you are still sick." He lowered the menu and stared at her.

Sara, I'm going to slice you up. Who told you to actually write to him!

Virginia moved in her chair unnerved. She would settle this with Sara later.

"Aren't you going to ask me what she said?"

"I don't need to know from others what my state of mind is like, I think I know myself well enough, Maestro."

Guglielmo put down the menu and pursed his lip, barely shaking his head. "I see you're feeling better, you're back to your old Ranieri self, jokes always ready. Good for you. Oh and don't be mad with Sara, she only wanted to help."

He showed her the chat on his phone.

She took a fleeting peek. "So?"

"You were the one who told her to let me know you were sick. Poor thing, she just did what you told her, Ranieri... She just wanted to defend the mystery woman..."

Virginia removed her glasses and put them down along with her cell phone. She slumped back in her chair and touched her forehead, abandoning all belligerent vague intentions towards Sara. She kept looking at the cell phone of the cellist. It was true that she didn't have any social profiles any longer, but it wasn't like she hadn't done some research on them since the day she'd left him. And it was true that she'd wanted him to know that she felt like crap. She'd felt worse after she'd read the insults from fans who'd lashed out with not-so-cute insults towards her. Fortunately, her identity had somehow not been revealed. Although she didn't understand how that had been possible, since her colleagues knew for sure that the mystery woman was her. Strange that no one had revealed it.

As if reading her mind, Guglielmo added: "I hope you appreciated how, with Jelena, we defended your identity. That was my first thought, I didn't want this thing to ruin your life."

She tried to change the subject.

"So, will you tell me what are the conditions for you to accept this gig? What was is it that you said? Oh, yes, that you need *guarantees*."

They lowered their gazes as the waiter arrived for orders.

"One piada crudo and mozzarella," Virginia ordered distractedly.

"Two. And a medium beer. What about you?" Guglielmo stared at her again, making her uncomfortable.

"Just water," Virginia answered him altered, then looked up at the waiter and politely added, "Thank you."

The Maestro scratched his chin. He had an unkempt beard, which for a perverse play of light made his emerald eyes stand out even more. The color crept overbearingly into Virginia's soul, who could not support the man's gaze. The silence was prolonged without Guglielmo looking uncomfortable.

What a pain in the ass... On the other hand, I'm not in front of the average man... what a drag....

He does it on purpose, he doesn't answer me and keeps staring at me to make me uncomfortable. If he thinks I'm going to give in, he's wrong.

"You know what I've learned?" he told her, seeing the plates arrive, "To savor the silence, as if it were good food. To enjoy it. Although I still prefer real food. But I have to admit that waiting is nice too. Ah, I wanted to tell you that since you made that mention, I ended up reading Bulgakov. As for me, I chose Shakespeare, I don't know if you noticed..."

"And what does Shakespeare have to do with anything?" She enquired.

"He, too, wrote for his Queen, as I did for you..."

Oh please, give me a break!

They began to eat, leaving their discussion on hold but still exchanging glances: Virginia was holding back her anger, while the Maestro kept observing her curiously.

"Mmm, this piada is tasty, good choice, it reminds me of the prosciutto your father made me taste... in Casciana," he said nostalgically and hinted at a smile, "Tuscan prosciutto is the best, of course, but as you say, you can make do with..."

"Stop it, Guglielmo," she cut in. She had had enough. "I'd say we're not here for a tasting lesson. So, these guarantees that you want?"

"The first is that you and I are committed to not fighting, and the second is music-related. My quartet can, for obvious reasons, play classical music, the point is that we don't want to play that kind of music; just contemporary, covers or our own."

"Why are you telling me these things? I understand that you and the Marquis are friends, no? Therefore, from you, I expect nothing more than what I have already heard."

"And from me, what do you expect?" He asked her, slyly.

She snorted, "That you keep your instrument at bay. I don't want any awkward situations with the Marquis and his guests. Understood? Enjoy your meal."

She got up, grabbed her things and went to the cashier to pay.

She turned back tand saw him leaning back in his chair, arm dangling, watching her.

She didn't look away. She would have liked to talk to him like the first time, but now it was all just memories, as distant as the Christmas days spent together.

Suddenly, he smiled to herself.

In the end, seeing you again was helpful, Maestro. You gave me an idea.

She hustled nack to the office and called her colleagues.

"Virginia with the suggestions, we're a bit up in the air...there's just not enough time...," Claudio informed her as she stepped into the meeting room.

"Don't worry, I've got this." She replied, her tone as sure as ever. "First thing to do, we need about thirty wicker baskets, cute and dainty. Spare no expense, pick out a variety of sizes. In fact, bring them in different sizes, and gather everything to jazz them up: ribbons, straw, bows, buttons. Let your creative juices flow—same color, different colors, small details, big ones. Fabric, wood, you name it.

Just get those baskets."

She then turned to Elisabetta and said: "Get on the phone. Tell Sandra she's taking over your client appointment, and have her report back to you on how it went. We're good for now; let's kickstart this *Marquis' Tour*!"

When the three of them came out of the meeting, she opened a new word sheet and jotted down the ideas in her head and in a couple of hours, outlined the travel route, including the Four Bows activities and concerts.

Elisabetta poked her head in through the doorway. "Virginia, I've got the hotel reservations sorted on the company's behalf, but they're asking for everyone's names and some form of ID."

Virginia couldn't help but reminisce about her father's lessons on organization. Back in the day, he'd insist on preparedness, a trait she had learned while just heading to school. He was both dad and mom to her, juggling tasks and sometimes forgetting the most mundane things, like buying notebooks or mistakenly picking up odd tools they had no clue about.

It was those experiences that had taught her that meticulous planning was key.

"You have ours, the others', ask Carolina, Siveri told me she has everything." She answered bordering on annoyance. Her assistants were still not used to solving certain trifles by themselves.

"I already did, but she won't turn them over to me."

She looked up at Elisabetta. "What do you mean?"

"She said she has to take care of it personally. What do I tell the hoteliers?"

Elisabetta had looked at her watch, because it was five to one and Elia was waiting for her. After all, Elia had become part of the SiVery family and Virginia didn't feel like depriving him of his mother. She huffed, "Go home. I got this."

"Thank you, Virgi. It's just that my mother-in-law had an a-"

"Don't worry! Run, or you'll miss your train. I'll see you tomorrow," she told her slipping on her jacket, "I'm going to see what's gotten into Carolina..." She rolled her eyes and Elisabetta laughed.

She then added, "Virgi, you're the best. I've printed and put in different folders, each reservation for each hotel; I'll leave them on your desk. You just need to forward the list of names and the relevant documents. I've been assured that everything else is fine. Ciao!"

Virginia gave her an approving nod and headed for the elevator. She waited a few minutes, then took the stairs, because she was impatient to know the reason why Carolina didn't want to cooperate with Elisabetta. Was it because of some gossip about her affair with the cellist?

When she arrived, Carolina was not there. "Damn, she's already gone home!" she exclaimed, not noticing that the door to the boss' office was slightly ajar.

"Carolina?" she heard call.

Phew! She looked up. "Ah, hello Mister Siveri, it's me." She tapped the door and walked in. "I was looking for Carolina, because I need the participants' papers for the de' Tomei field trip."

Siveri observed her. He was sitting next to the glass table, which he used to receive customers, and invited her to sit down. "Come in." He moved the chair, which Virginia had wanted to buy for herself as well, but at that moment associated with the torture chair of the inquisition. She could do nothing but sit down, "Yes, about those papers..."

"Carolina won't be able to provide them," he said resolutely, and Virginia leaned forward. "I beg your pardon? We can't complete the reservations without them!" She had raised her tone a little.

"The Marquis was very clear. He has sent everything to my attention, asking to keep the names of the guests and the, let's say sensitive information, strictly confidential. Turn over to me the name of the hotel where you will be staying and we will take care of everything from here, including your documents and those of the group. I asked to have Carolina keep everything otherwise there is a risk of confusion. She will make herself available for the entire duration of the trip."

"And what am I supposed to call the guests if I don't know their names?"

"The Marquis has thought of that too," he said handing her a sheet of paper, "Here are the names of the participants. Obviously, they're nicknames, but it's fun... Besides, he did a great job, with each photo he associated the nickname, so you'll know exactly who you're talking to. Keep it, I have a copy."

"Lila, Nero, Titti, Conte, Nelly, Bardo, Mimi, Lallo, Vera, Alfy! These are the names I'm supposed to call them by?"

"I told you the Marquis is a funny guy!"

"So I won't know who he is..."

"No, he's very particular about confidentiality. Consider that not even Carolina has this privilege. The identity documents are secret and only I have the password to open them and I will send it exclusively to the manager of the hotel we have chosen. In fact, tell me who it is, because I will have to call him personally."

"You'll have to make more than on phone call, I'm afraid."

CHAPTER 17.

The alarm clock had gone off very early. The suit she used when she had to go on long trips was waiting for her ironed on the crutch, hanging on the closet door.

The inevitable jacket and *palazzo* pants. She absolutely wanted to make a good impression on her new client, the Marquis. She touched a dress that Guglielmo had bought her. Armani, black, soft. It was the warmest of those he had found for her. Maybe he had chosen it for when they were supposed to return to Milan together.

To hell with it!

She decided to take it with her.

After all, it was very suitable for the nobility. She dressed as she went over the list of attendees. She had placed the paper on the bed and was looking at the pictures. Who knows what nickname the Marquis had given himself. Bardo? Lallo? There were five couples and among the women was his fiancée. Lila? Vera?

The appointment was set in the center of Milan, at the Grand Hotel de la Ville. The director had allowed her, for a large fee, to rent one of the meeting rooms for the entire day, in order to gather the guests and organize the departure by car for the early afternoon.

She ate a sandwich at noon and arrived at the hotel wearing her usual Chanel purse and a suitcase. It was one of the Vuitton's Guglielmo had given her.

"Hi Martina. Are they here?"

"Yes, all of them. Claudio is getting them set up in the various limousines as well as getting their bags and stuff loaded into the vans. However, not everyone wants to take our cars." She pointed toward Guglielmo, who was practically lying on one of the white ottomans as he was intent on looking at his cell phone. Every now and then he giggled. Every once in a while he'd type something. He was dressed with a T-shirt and jeans. A jacket tossed to the side.

Martina clarified, "He said he prefers to drive himself. He's waiting for directions about the address."

"All right," Virginia answered her, "Take my bag outside and make sure it gets taken. Here, I'll take care of it." She stared at the cellist annoyed.

Didn't he have anything better to wear?

"The rest, you said, is already all in there, isn't it?"

"Yes, but let me check again to make sure!" exclaimed Martina, grabbing her suitcase and heading out in a hurry.

Virginia approached the cellist, cautiously. She would have liked to stroke his hair, but merely brushed his arm. His eyes stared at her absently.

"We have to go."

"I'll come with mine," he answered her. He picked up his jacket.

"No, I prefer to travel all together. It's for an insurance-related issue."

Claudio rushed in. "Virginia, Virginia, good thing you got here! There was a mix-up with the limos and vans!"

"What do you mean?"

"There's not enough vans for everyone."

"Claudio, that's impossible, I was the one who organized the logistics. I've checked several times. Do the count again. Nucci is coming too."

"Oh, come on, Ranieri, don't you ever get it wrong? Don't you ever take a blunder?" the cellist's voice dripped with sarcasm.

"Guglielmo, be good," she shot back sharply.

"Um," Claudio said, "I've already counted. I'm sure. At this point, I guess someone has to stay here, I can stay..."

"Absolutely, not! You're needed," Virginia exclaimed. "Let me make a call and we'll work something out."

"The solution is right in front of you, Ranieri,"

said determined the Maestro. "Go ahead, Claudio. Virginia and I will come to Tuscany with my car."

"Don't even think about it—" Virginia began but Claudio interrupted her and ran towards Guglielmo shouting, "Thank you, Maestro! Thank you! Virginia, we're leaving then, as we're already late, we'll see you both there!"

"Claudio, get back here now!" She screamed angrily, but he had already disappeared into one of the vans. She made to reach him, but Guglielmo grabbed her wrist.

"Don't touch me!" She cried out and he obeyed, but a half laugh escaped him. "Ouch!"

She then walked briskly toward the exit of the hotel, cell phone to her ear.

"They've already left," Guglielmo told her, "and you know as well as I do that it would take the rental company a half hour before they'd get another car in. That's if all goes well and if they have another one ready. Besides, it's not like I'm going to eat you."

He waved the car keys in her face. "So, shall we go?"

"Yes, but this time, I'm driving." She forcefully took the keys and added, "So? Where's the Porsche?"

"There is no way you're driving. Give me back the keys..." he told her forcing himself to be gentle.

"Come on, Maestro, let's not waste any more time. What was it you said? No fights between us, right? So, don't make me any more angry than I already am. Here, I'm in charge. Get your stuff. Where did you park?"

"Around the Corner..."

They left the hotel and went to where the 911 was parked. Virginia opened the trunk, waited for Guglielmo to load his trolley and sat down to drive. She put the key in the dashboard, while he, sitting next to her, was already adjusting the seat back, to make his legs more comfortable. His presence dominated the interior of the cockpit in an overpowering way: with his good scent, with his gestures.

Virginia intended to avoid any involvement and vowed not to speak, but Guglielmo broke immediately the silence..

"So Ranieri, this is a special car, you have to treat it right."

She didn't wait for him to continue his explanations and started the engine, aiming her eyes at him, fiery, "Nucci, I can drive a car."

"Yes, but this one is not like all the others..."

"Strange that you should be the one to say that, since to you one woman is as good as another. You treat them all the same. Without a shred of sensitivity."

The Maestro rested his hands on the dashboard, arms outstretched, and shook his head, huffing.

"Alright, alright..." he said more to himself, as if trying to calm himself down. He turned his head towards Virginia, and continued to explain, punctuating the words as if he were talking to someone who did not know Italian: "This car has a seven-speed manual transmission and when you shift down, you have to be careful, because it is done on purpose; it is a system that automatically starts the accelerator, to allow a smoother change. Do you understand?"

Ah jeez, he is even more handsome, when he is angry, she thought.

The soul might have doubted, but Virginia's body was determined, so she continued to stare at him blankly. He glared at her, too, and Virginia, out of spite, shifted into neutral, and gave gas. Twice. The engine made a powerful noise, but Guglielmo's voice echoed more forcefully inside: "Virginia!"

Devilish smile and sarcastic reply: "What did you say, Maestro? The engine needs to be revved up, doesn't it?"

"You're impossible!" he told her.

"Yeah, whatever, let's go go." Shift to first gear, start. In jerks.

I can drive, I can drive, I can drive. So what if

I drive a Toyota Aygo, automatic, though! A car is a car! She told herself.

"Virginia, pull over, please..." Broad nod with his hand. Furious.

"Be good Maestro..."

"I said, pull over!"

"Are you afraid I'm going to break it? There are plenty of other Porsches, aren't there? Like there are plenty of other women."

Moment of hesitation before muttering, "Okay, you always win...if you break it, I'll give it to you."

"Ha, ha, ha..."

Guglielmo seemed to calm down, while Virginia, although she was making an effort to appear invulnerable, was actually agitated, because she was not used to driving a sports car like that. And certainly not with Guglielmo at her side. Out of the corner of her eye she saw him fiddling with the display, but she didn't take her eyes off the windshield, she couldn't be distracted.

The interior dashboard lights came on. Greens. John Legend's music in the background. The navigation system with the map.

"If you tell me the address..." He brushed her arm, with which he held the change, and she reacted stymied, "Guglielmo. We have four hours ahead of us. Don't start. It's hard enough as it is. Anyway, I know where I'm going. I don't need your navigator!"

Translation: I'm getting on with my life, I can do it without you. Maybe. Don't cry, don't cry, don't cry, damn it!

She had pretended to pose as the confident, unscathed woman, but she wasn't.

Suddenly she was jealous, too. I wonder who he's with now. That blonde he was hanging out with on New Year's Eve?

She continued driving with her vision fogged.

"Stop, I'll drive" His tone was gentle. He handed her a handkerchief, which she took with a nervous gesture.

Silence. Engine and music together. She continued driving.

Guglielmo spoke again. "When you disappeared, in Dubai, at first I thought you were preparing a surprise for me." He chuckled, "In fact, your departure was quite unexpected."

Silence. She pushed on the accelerator and Guglielmo moved forward, trying to scan her face. Virginia felt his eyes straight onto hers, but she remained staring at the road in front of her. They arrived at the toll booth.

"I've got the telepass, head for that lane..." His arm just rested on hers. And she didn't fight back.

"Virginia whatever I said or did wrong, I'm sorry. I truly am."

Silence.

He continued: "Did you know that two weeks ago your boss came with his wife to see us at La Scala? We talked about you. He is very pleased with the way you work, he really appreciates your professionalism, your meticulousness. He told me about the acid green napkin. That you had found all the accessories in the exact same shade. And then, at that moment, I flashed and realized what the numbers you blather on and on about like you're a crazy person mean. They're the numbers associated with the colors, you need them to find the same shade. Right?"

Yes, that's right, like your eyes: Pantone green number 348. No other eyes are as intense as yours. Or handsome. Contrary to what she was thinking, she replied sarcastically, "Very good. And bravo to our *Guglielmino*. Always smart."

Who in the heck gave permission to Siveri to talk about me anyway?

"Ha, ha, ha! You know who used to call me that? *Guglielmino*? My grandmother Vittoria. When she was mad at me. No one else but the two of you."

"Uh, wow, what a coincidence..."

"Are you seeing someone these days? Maybe that Filippo guy?"

"Let's be clear, Nucci, my dating situation is none of your business as of January 1st of this year."

"I don't have anyone." He answered her as if

she had asked, and Virginia turned to look at him with a confused expression.

What do you want to tell me, Nucci?

He went on in a tone of voice she knew well: a tone of self commiseration. "When I realized you weren't coming back, I felt terrible. My stomach was in pieces. I swear. I was in bed for two whole days. That had never happened to me before. The day I was finally able to get up, I did as you told me. I took your advice and confided in a friend. Due to a series of events that I'll explain another time, fortunately I had the opportunity... he was with me."

He paused for a moment as if to ponder and said, "I mean, I finally talked to my brother. And I have to say, Ranieri..."

He looked at her and she instinctively turned back to him, who continued mournfully, "...that it didn't do any fucking good..."

Virginia didn't hold back a small laugh.

"Oh right, go ahead and make fun of me as you always do..." he said.

"I didn't mean to. It made me laugh the way you said it," she answered him bluntly, regretting it immediately.

The Maestro's lips pursed the way she liked them.

Stop it, Nucci...

"Anyway, two days later I went back to Milan.

Coriolan was very worried and cancelled the first two dates. Then I had to resume playing. But things just weren't it the same again."

The music continued and they didn't speak again until they reached their destination. Occasionally they said half words to each other. A few sidelong glances. Virginia was overwhelmed by the talk. By him.

She decided she would tell him why she left. Maybe Sara was right and it would be good for her. However, not in the car, not while she was driving a two hundred thousand euro sports car. When she parked, she quickly got out and walked around the car and stood in front of Guglielmo the instant he got out. She looked at him and felt that the attraction between them had not diminished. That cheeky expression on Guglielmo's face enveloped her, making her feel desired. Like the words he said to her, velvety, persuasive, with a light snap of his tongue, "You know I recognized this outfit, don't you? I picked them out myself as well as the other clothes and accessories... I did it before I left to come at your dad's place at Christmas."

Did you really pick out the pashminas as well? Did you really already organize for Dubai?

"It felt good, because I was thinking of you as I touched the fabrics. Soft like your skin..."

Virginia glanced sidelong at the arm muscle

leaning against the door and decided that her moment
of truth had arrived.

"Guglielmo, do you have any idea how I felt
when I got back to the hotel suite and saw you with
that blonde?!" Voice choked, eyes veiled by tears. She
clenched her fists, for strength. She was ready for the
train of excuses he would have listed for her, but
instead he brushed her shoulder, that slow movement,
that rubbing that she liked.

Oh, my God, Nucci, stop it....

All of a sudden the cellist appeared relieved.

"Ranieri, you finally said it!" The usual smile,
forelock on his forehead and the other hand on his
shoulder as well. "We can take it from here. I want to
tell you right away that you have every reason to be
angry. In fact, it should have been a surprise, but I
was wrong not to warn you. *Mea culpa.*"

She tried to move, annoyed. "You don't think
you can include me in your threesomes, do you! Who
do you take me for!"

In all response the cellist slammed the door of
the car and looked at her straight in the eyes before
answering.

"I don't do such things, Ranieri, and above all
I would never allow myself to make fun of anyone. I
would never make fun of you, never. You're
obviously not ready or willing to know the truth yet
and at this point, there's nothing I can do about it.

Now just give me back my keys and lead the way."

To Virginia, he looked and sounded genuinely offended. Which she thought was bizarre.

CHAPTER 18.

The entire group arrived at the Borgo San Giuliano, a five star luxury resort nestled in the heart of Tuscany, under the cover of night; a late-hour arrival that demanded a quiet, solitary dinner in each of the guest's villa—a thoughtful touch Virginia had orchestrated. Her designated abode was the *Vecchio Forno*, christened after an old bread oven that stood as a relic within the renovated farmhouse turned luxury haven. Despite the stone walls and terracotta floors, the villa exuded a warmth that seeped through the carefully chosen fabrics, enveloping her in a cozy ambiance. As soon as she opened the door Virginia felt wrapped in a romantic embrace. And her first thought was of Guglielmo's arms.

Determined not to think about him, she indulged in a bath intended for pure relaxation, perched atop stone stairs overlooking the illuminated entrance, where rows of iconic Tuscan cypress trees stood in sentinel-like vigil. The tub filled with cascading bubbles as she eased into the warm waters, setting her glasses aside on a nearby stool and releasing the knot in her hair, letting it cascade freely.

She still had his scent on her and hesitated before stepping into the water. A long breath to calm himself and foot into the water. The phone vibrated.

"What is it now?" she told herself, reluctantly taking her device, fearful that it might have been some hiccup to be worked out.

She scrolled and read:

[Whatsapp message from Guglielmo Nucci].
Nice relais. Tomorrow morning I'll wait for you for breakfast. Half past seven. Good night, Ranieri.

Virginia shook her head.

No, my dear Nucci, You clearly haven't understood. You can wait forever in the breakfast room. I'm not taking any orders from you or anyone for that matter.

She was about to respond when a new message came in.

[Whatsapp message from Guglielmo Nucci].
Before you go berserk on me about breakfast: Cori wants to meet so as to know where we're going to play, acoustics, arrangements etc.. So yes, I guess it'll be a threesome after all, like you mentioned....

A half-smile escaped her and she murmured,

"All right, Nucci. This is war."

[Whatsapp message to Guglielmo Nucci].

Agree to meet in the morning. Speaking of games, it seems to me that in your little notes you called me queen. Not once, but one hundred and forty-eight times, if I'm not mistaken? So, since I am a queen, you should also know that I do not play games reserved for clowns. I leave those to you.

She immersed herself completely in the tub, satisfied with what she had written.

The phone in the room rang. Fortunately, there was also one near the tub. She pressed the button, without picking up the handset. "Yes?"

"Ms. Ranieri, there's a guest asking for you."

"Now? Can't it wait?" Her sentence was cut short by a strange noise. "Hello? Hello?"

Then came the doorbell. Oh no, not now, she said, hoping it wasn't Claudio or Elisabetta summoning her with some urgent issue.

"Just a minute."

Swiftly stepping out of the tub, she dried herself hurriedly, slipping on her glasses to set the tone, as a persistent knocking continued at the door.

"I'm coming, I'm coming! No need to tear the door down!" She slipped on her robe and walked down the stone stairs in her bare feet.

"What is it? What's wrong?" She opened the door without thinking and found Guglielmo in front of her.

She mumbled surprised: "What do you want?"

"One hundred and forty-nine," he replied, leaning his hands against the doorframe. In that way he towered over her, but Virginia continued to look at him and just shook her head, "One hundred and forty-nine what?"

"I called you Queen one hundred and forty-nine times. Including when we did it in the walk-in closet, in Dubai." He stared at her seriously. "Ah, just so you know, I bought that mirror." His right hand came down further on the doorframe, at Virginia's shoulder level, and she looked down at his fingers and said, "Whatever, so what? The substance doesn't change."

"The woman you saw in the suite was my sister."

"Well that's a relief!" huffed Virginia and crossed her arms. "And the other one as well? She was your sister too?"

"Well, in a way..." He said smiling.

"Oh please, Guglielmo!" Virginia closed the door.

"Virginia, wait!"

"Please leave or I'll call the front desk." She

said from behind the door.

She saw him leave.

Nucci, she sighed. A tear came out of her right eye.

CHAPTER 19.

That night, Virginia's dreams were also taken over by the cellist, and when the alarm clock rang she felt like she hadn't been able to get enough rest.

She picked up her cell phone.

[Whatsapp message from Guglielmo Nucci].
Good morning, my Queen. Last night, I told you the truth. I understand that you need a more thorough explanation. MGPMCdT.

Virginia responded in a rush.

[Whatsapp message to Guglielmo Nucci].
Yes, and also for your posts. Stop the cat you have in your bed to randomly push buttons....

[Whatsapp message from Guglielmo Nucci].
LOL...Ranieri, I miss you.

"I miss you too..." she whispered, but sent no reply.

Perched on the bed, she scrolled through those

messages once more. The lingering fear of reopening the heartaches she had painstakingly mended was overwhelming. Despite the cellist's attempts to reconnect, she resolved to convince herself that keeping distance was the wisest course until the trip's end. However, a pivotal appointment with him lay ahead, a test to the resolution she had just made.

She swiftly messaged Claudio and Martina, delegating the responsibility of tending to the Marquis and his entourage while she ensured the arrangements for the Four Bows' concert were flawless, as meticulously organized. But before diving into her duties, she made her way to the tree room for the breakfast meeting with Guglielmo and Cori.

The space exuded the same inviting warmth as the rooms, with wooden tables and rounded seating. A mighty oak tree dominated the center, showcasing its gnarled trunk, while decorative plants draped from its highest branches, perfectly complementing the green tablecloths below.

Cori sat by the huge plant and admired the tuscan countryside through the large windows.

"Virginia," he stood up as soon as he saw her. "How are you?"

"Very well thank you and you? And Jelena?"

"She's been a little more tired lately, you know with the kids... but it will pass! Guglielmo doesn't know the place where we're supposed to play so I asked him to meet us. In my opinion-"

"You're right, yes," she interrupted him, "After breakfast I have to go there, to see that they've fixed everything."

She looked around, but there was no sign of the Maestro. She sat down across from Cori and he started talking about the family.

"Ferenc and Anna give us a lot of trouble, but you want to know something? And look I never thought I'd say this until I had them. I couldn't do without them anymore. In fact, I'd like another kid, but Jelena isn't much for it." He laughed and changed the subject by talking about acoustics and sound, but Virginia continued to eat and giving smiles of circumstance, not really listening to him. She was thinking that it had been a mistake to have agreed to organize that outing. By now she was in the game and she wouldn't back out, but she couldn't help thinking that she would see Guglielmo for two more days, after which their paths would separate forever. The wound in her heart opened again.

At one point, she stood up. "Cori, let's go. Is it just you or do the others have to come too?"

"No, no, just Guglielmo and I."

Yes, that's who I meant, she thought.

"In fact, odd that he's not already here..." Cori added.

"All right, we'll do without him," Virginia said, comforted, though her soul wasn't quite happy.

It's for the better.

The van was already waiting for them with the doors open and the driver helped the two of them load the instruments. "Sorry Virginia," Cori looked awkward, "it's just that I need to feel the effect of each bow, to decide on the best arrangement. Of course if Guglielmo had been here, I would have done it sooner." He loaded the cello.

"I don't know if you're going to be able to play that one," she said, pointing to Guglielmo's instrument.

"Well, yes, it's true I don't play it... However, since there's room, I need it for the arrangement on stage."

"No problem, Cori. I've kept the car lot on purpose. The location is close and we can stay as long as you need."

In fact, it took them less than ten minutes to get to the Abbey of San Galgano. More precisely, at the foot of Monte Siepi, in the place where the Abbey stood.

"What church is it?" asked Cori curiously as they crossed the vast lawn that surrounded the abbey. The February sun illuminated the walls with a soft light and made the stones of the façade alive and redder and instead those on the sides, which made up those thin pointed perturbations, alternated, now light, now dark, in a game of reverberations that contributed to making the church, in Virginia's eyes, beautiful.

"It's the abbey of San Galgano, it doesn't have a roof..."

"A bit of a ruin, isn't it?"

Virginia looked at him sternly and Cori tried to apologize, "I mean, no, she's undoubtedly beautiful, but..."

"Around the twenties," she tried to explain, "the state declared it a protected asset and since then it has been used for performances, exhibitions. Concerts. Its characteristic is that it has these high Gothic walls, but no ceiling. I thought it might be a striking location..."

"Yes, let's hope it doesn't rain..."

"Fingers crossed."

They entered the abbey. The workers were already at work and had brought inside the chairs, the red carpet to cover the beaten earth floor and the fifteen or so mushroom heaters that Virginia had brought in to dampen the cold of the evening during the concert.

"Oh, look," exclaimed Cori, "Guglielmo is here after all!"

They saw him, at the back of the abbey, talking smilingly with the workers who were laying out the carpet. He bent down with three of them and they walked down the aisle unrolling the mantle.

"What is he doing?" laughed Cori, and then turning to him, shouted, "Hey, Giglielmo, looking for a career change?"

The cellist exchanged a few words with the man next to him and then walked towards them. He was smiling.

He opened his arms wide, pulling Virginia into an unexpected embrace, spinning her around in an impromptu dance. She instinctively glanced upward at the sky.

"Thank you, Ranieri, thank you, this is truly a magical place!"

"Put me down Nucci! And mind you, I'm not doing this for you, I'm doing it for the Marquis. Down, I said."

"I know, I know, but I'm very happy too. Here, down you go..."

Her feet touched the ground again and a fond smile escaped Virginia; she couldn't help but be overwhelmed by that happiness.

Stop it! Immediately! She told herself.

William touched his forelock, "Cori, tell me you have an extra violin! Please! I didn't know the concert was going to be held here and I wanted to see this place again and..."

"Not only do I have the violin, but I also have

your beloved cello, my friend!"

"Cori! I'll make you a monument!" he patted him on the back and ran outside.

The violist coughed and looked at Virginia. "Well, that means he'll help me out..."

Guglielmo returned with the cello. "I'll start, then you tell me." The euphoria was contagious and Cori cheerfully replied, "Yes, yes, I'm coming!"

Cori lowered his voice and approached Virginia again, "Thank goodness! It's been over a month since I've seen him this happy-" He quickly corrected himself. "Er, sorry Virginia, I meant-."

"Yes, don't worry, I understand. It's nice." She smiled and added, "I've got some things to take care of. I'll see you later," and she disappeared into the back of the van. She leaned against the seat and breathed, tense.

The cellist's behavior was incomprehensible, but most of all what she didn't understand was why she was still, despite everything, under his spell.

Enough, Ranieri, pull yourself together!

She admired the merino wool and cashmere blankets she had personally purchased from Tiffany's. The clear cellophane made the T&Co 1837 logo visible.

"You clearly have a penchant for numbers." a voice said.

Him again.

"Don't you have to rehearse, Maestro?" she asked without turning around and arranging the blankets two by two to bring them inside the abbey.

"Here, let me help you with these blankets first. They're nice..."

"For your friend, the Marquis."

"Have you met him?" he asked her.

She shook her head, saying nothing. She needed to talk to him as little as possible, and she had already let herself go a little too much before.

"And aren't you curious to meet him? I'll introduce you if you want."

She had to answer.

"No, thank you. The Marquis has set up this outing asking for the utmost secrecy, and it's enough for me to know that everything is going smoothly. I hope I've anticipated everything."

"Did you anticipate me too?" He gave her his usual mischievous smile, this time, however, the small wrinkle, near his eye, lengthened.

Nervous, Nucci?

The cellist grabbed five blankets and walked toward the abbey, whistling. "I'll be back for the others. Leave it to me, Ranieri. I'll put them on the chairs, then you place them as you think best, you being so good."

They stayed at the abbey all morning, but did not speak again. Virginia had her hands full moving the chairs around so that everyone had the best possible view, as well as the warmth of the heaters, and she gave precise instructions to the workers on how to arrange the lights that were to go up between the bays. They worked accompanied by music. It was magnificent.

The abbey echoed with music, melodies filling the space interrupted by playful notes, even the occasional whistle tossed between the musicians to signify pauses or transitions. Unintentionally, Virginia frequently found herself glancing at Guglielmo, and without fail, his gaze met hers—sometimes tender, at times penetrating, but always brimming with intensity.

After the workers left, Virginia sat down and, leaning her head on her arm, stood watching the two musicians take turns at the strings and discuss pointing out the best spots in the church to stand.

"Ranieri!" the cellist shouted to her, "We need you."

"Ah, yes Virginia, if you don't mind, thank you!" pressed Cori.

"All right..." She stood up, but the cellist ran toward her. "No, no, just sit." He grabbed a blanket and tore off the cellophane.

"No, Guglielmo! What are you doing, they are for this evening."

He smiled as he placed the blanket on her lap.

Their faces were close, their breaths overlapped, and their gazes stayed searching for each other longer than expected.

"Now close your eyes Virginia and listen." He murmured. "This time, I'll play just for you. And there will be no Ranieri, who will be able to stop me."

Their mouths seemed to touch, but the Maestro straightened up, turning back to Cori, and Virginia covered her face, partly to hide the blush she knew was on her cheeks.

The two musicians began to play music she had never heard. Sublime. She raised her head and opened her eyes. The blue sky above the abbey enveloped her completely, as the notes swirled around her, making her hoist herself higher and higher into heaven.

"It's beautiful!"

When the music finished, the subtle happiness that had pervaded her and reflected on her face did not leave her until they were in the van. They traveled seated across from each other, with Cori who couldn't stop talking about how happy Ferenc would be to see the mythical sword in the stone that lay in the nearby museum and the fact that he would definitely plan a trip with his family soon.

Guglielmo smiled and typed something on his phone. He looked at Virginia and indicated her purse.

Virginia lowered her head and reached for her

cell phone.

[Whatsapp message from Guglielmo Nucci].
Ranieri, I have decided that from now on I will only play for you.

[Whatsapp message to Guglielmo Nucci].
Fine. Except for tonight and tomorrow.

[Whatsapp message from Guglielmo Nucci].
If it's just you, sure.

[Whatsapp message to Guglielmo Nucci].
Don't joke, Guglielmo. It won't just be me and you know it.

She looked at him sternly and heard the phone vibrate.

[Whatsapp message from Guglielmo Nucci].
I'm not kidding, Ranieri.

[Whatsapp message to Guglielmo Nucci].
I have also arranged everything for tomorrow at the Tepidarium in Florence. You don't want to displease the Marquis now, do you?

[Whatsapp message from Guglielmo Nucci].

Great location. What about the baskets? When are you going to put them up? And what will they contain? I'm curious.

[Whatsapp message to Guglielmo Nucci].
Tomorrow at the botanical garden. They're picnic baskets, with those Tuscan delicacies you like so much. Hey, who told you about the baskets?

They arrived at the Borgo and so the conversation was interrupted. Guglielmo came out, picked up his cello and waved goodbye. He seemed to be in a hurry.

"See you later!" said Cori.

When the time came for everyone to go to the abbey together, a problem seemed to have arisen. The fact was that Virginia had planned for the concert to take place before dinner, to avoid the cold night, but there was no sign of Guglielmo. The Maestro seemed to have disappeared.

"Virginia what do we do?" Claudio asked, "The guests are all already in the limos..."

"Virginia I'm sorry!" It was Cori. "We don't know where he is. Jànos and Tamas have been trying to call him for half an hour." He pointed to one fiddler who was pacing back and forth, cell phone in hand, and the other who was next to him, who, seeing them, spread his arms wide.

What are you doing, Nucci?! Don't you want to play in front of your friends?! If you're trying to win me back, you've got the wrong strategy!

She looked at her watch, it was six thirty and she couldn't waste time keeping up with the cellist's whims.

"Cori, have you three ever played without him?" she asked the violist.

"Yes, but..."

"Then we will apologize to the guests and tell them that Guglielmo is not feeling well and he will not be part of the concert tonight. As for tomorrow," she turned to Martina, "we'll find a backup cellist. Go make some calls, please."

Virginia looked at the horizon, the hills, the olive trees. The cellist had disappeared with his Porsche. No messages, no nothing.

CHAPTER 20.

As night fell, the entire group gathered at San Galgano. Virginia simmered with anger, her frustration aimed at Guglielmo for disrupting her meticulously planned event and potentially sabotaging a promising relationship with the firm's new client, the Marquis de' Tomei. She still hadn't a clue who this marquis was; his absence intrigued her. How would he arrive at San Galgano if all the cars were taken? These nobles, she mused, they truly thrive on extravagance.

Overlooking the abbey, the radiant full moon heightened the already magical atmosphere. Leading the guests towards the entrance, Virginia was halted by Cori. "Please, Virginia, you enter first and lead the way."

She nodded and stepped forward, entering the abbey. Lights illuminated the stage, drawing attention to a man seated at the center. Her heart sank at the familiar sight.

Nucci. What in the world?

"Hello, Virginia. Please, take a seat in front of me."

As she entered, Virginia hadn't realized the seating arrangement had been altered. Now, there was only one chair placed before the stage, leaving all others behind.

She stood in bewildered confusion as the other guests filtered in, each taking a seat behind her.

"Hold on, I'm lost. What's happening? Where's the Marquis? What's he going to say?" Virginia's questions fell into the ether as a small group of guests approached her—a trio comprising two women and a man. One of the women, with long, silky black hair, struck a chord of recognition within Virginia. She was the same woman from the hotel in Dubai!

Another woman, also with long hair but a honey-colored hue, joined the scene. These were the two women Guglielmo had been with. What was going on here?

The woman with oriental features and black hair gestured to a man, previously unnoticed by Virginia amid her confusion. He rose from his seat and approached her with a warm smile.

"Pleasure to meet you. I am Marquis Adelchi Giorgio Paolo Maria Casarinucci de' Tomei."

He bore a striking resemblance to Nucci... less muscular, though. It was no wonder she found him familiar.

"Good evening, Marquis," she said shyly and

a bow came naturally to her. "I was under the impression your name was Manfredi..." Virginia ventured, a flurry of thoughts clouding her mind, leaving her bewildered.

The Marquis offered a warm smile and spoke kindly, "Manfredi is my brother. He's mentioned you quite a bit. We nearly crossed paths in Dubai. Come, allow me to introduce you to my wife, Lin, and my sister, Marquise Agnese Beatrice Vittoria Maria."

Virginia offered another half-bow, and the Marquis's wife, Lin, greeted her with a nod and a smile. Meanwhile, Adelchi continued, his voice serene, "Your expression suggests my brother hasn't mentioned my sister Agnese and me. He promised he would, the scoundrel."

"I'm a bit lost," Virginia murmured, genuinely confused as the pieces of a surprising puzzle started to click together.

Adelchi glanced at Agnes, prompting Virginia to realize the implication. If she's Manfredi's sister, then that means...

Her gaze returned to the stage where the cellist, wearing a smile and nodding in her direction, waited. "So Manfredi is..." she began, the question trailing off. Feeling unsteady, she sought some form of support, but the ground beneath her seemed to give way, leaving her stepping back in disbelief.

Manfredi is-not even the mind could

pronounce the name.

The Marquis Adelchi came to her aid: "I believe that he introduced himself to you with the name of Guglielmo. I always told my father that he shouldn't have given him the title. Too rebellious! But, you know how it is, births are what they are... Just kidding. In fact, we even inherited the title of nobility from our great-grandparents. The thing is, my father has imposed a certain amount of caution on us in revealing who we really are to the whole world, so we use made-up names. That is, in the sense that we have chosen our middle names and part of one of the surnames. For example, my name is Giorgio Nucci and my sister, Beatrice. Instead, Manfredi is Guglielmo. Unlike me and Agnese, Manfredi is even more shrewd and reserved because of the profession he has chosen and the notoriety he has achieved. My father is not very happy. As he gets older, he's getting better, but Manfredi's fame worries him. Although it must be admitted that his entourage manages to ensure the anonymity that our family demands. Only a few people get to know the truth."

The Maestro was now coming down from the stage to greet her. And Virginia let out a convulsive, almost hysterical laugh. Definitely liberating.

He made her a deep bow and said sternly: "Manfredi Guglielmo Pietro Maria Casarinucci de' Tomei, to serve you, Miss Ranieri. In fact, I'm about to go and play a *serenata* for my girlfriend. Will you sit and watch?"

Past the moment of hilarity, Virginia looked at him in disbelief. "You mean to tell me that you arranged this whole Marquis Tour, for... for me?"

The pursed lips on the cellist's face were more than enough of an answer for her.

Virginia switched from sheer disbelief to a more altered intonation, "Why didn't you tell me your brothers were coming to Dubai? Now I can explain the suite being so big..."

"You didn't give me time. My brother, with Lin, and my sister Beatrice were scheduled to arrive that day. I wanted you to meet them, after I had told you about them in Casciana. I was a fool not to tell you sooner. I meant to surprise you, but that morning, I was overwrought from the concert and didn't think Adelchi would arrive before lunch, but he was the one who surprised me..."

He looked at his brother. "I think you saw Adelchi, Lin and Beatrice... and I don't know, maybe you thought it was me, along with someone else..."

I'm afraid so...

"Weren't you wearing glasses?" He said laughing.

I had them, I had them, along with a heavy dose of tears.

"Well, I..." explained Virginia "...I opened the

door and saw the two of them by the pool, and the next thing I knew, you came in. And she, she gave you a kiss!" She pointed her finger at Agnes, but immediately retracted it blushing. "Guglielmo's back was turned, I thought... I'm sorry, I was confused... the virago kept poking me and I really thought..." she justified herself to the other two as well.

Manfredi laughed as he commented. "The virago?"

"Adriana."

"Ah, but then you were jealous..." The cellist smiled slyly. "You don't have to be," he added quickly, tone detached "I left her."

"Oh, I'm sorry. And why did you wait so long to tell me the truth about them?"

"Virginia, I didn't know why you had left me. I thought you'd gotten back together with that Filippo guy... It wasn't until Sara wrote me that I realized the misunderstanding..." He looked at her sister.

Agnes stood up approaching Virginia. "I remember giving my brother a kiss. On the cheek," she pointed out haughtily. "With my brothers, we see each other very little. This time in Dubai, thanks to you." She walked around her studying her. "Manfredi seems very much in love this time."

Virginia turned purple and murmured, "I'm so sorry..."

The siblings laughed, but she was

embarrassed, and most of all, she didn't know how to deal with Guglielmo a.k.a. Manfredi a.k.a. the Marquis. She wanted him, but still feared to let go. She was in the grip of conflicting feelings. This time, it was Agnese who came to her rescue, because she added, in a sweeter tone: "Frankly, I have never seen Manfredi reduced this way for a woman. After you left, we struggled to get him back on track, he was very sick... And he kept saying that by now you had gotten into his head..."

Virginia wrinkled her forehead and turned to Manfredi: "Nucci, Nucci, Nucci... or rather Marquis Manfredi... See how I was right? It will take me a long time to fix you..." She had resumed the ironic tone with which she treated him, hoping he would notice, and he did, because he stepped forward, saying, "My Ranieri, she's finally back and I want you to take all the time you need, to tune me up..." He hugged her tightly and Virginia offered no resistance and let go in turn, squeezing her shoulders, her waist, her back tightly.

"I missed you."

"I missed you too..." Tears ran from her eyes.

"I'm sorry Virginia, I really am. I'm in love with you, I'd do anything for you. I want you and you?" he murmured taking her face in his hands, strong.

Virginia laughed, wiping away her tears.

"Well, Nucci, since I know your secret identity now, I guess I have no alternative, right? If not, I'm afraid you'll have to kill me..."

In that moment, Guglielmo enveloped her in an embrace, leaning in for a kiss that she didn't resist in the least. If anything, she had yearned for that kiss more than anything else in her life. Lost in the depth of his emerald green eyes, the cheers and applause from those around them faded into the background.

Don't miss the other books from Maddi Magrì already available at Amazon!

Giulia's Vineyard
(Italian Romance Stories Vol.1)

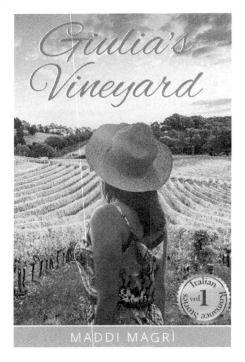

A new beginning. This is what Giulia needs after Paolo and her marriage are taken away from her. And to start over, Giulia leaves Milan and moves to the Marches region in central Italy. There, among rolling hills filled with sunflowers and vineyards, she meets Luca, a charming and witty winemaker. But he, too, has a past to forget.

Will he be the right person for a new chapter in her life?

A love in Milan
(Italian Romance Stories Vol.2)

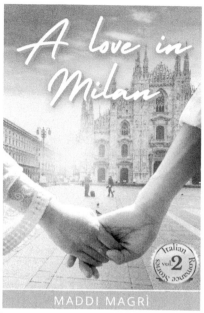

David would have recognized her anywhere in the world. Although years had passed, he would have recognized her face, her perfume, among a thousand others. Francesca was for him like a painting by Botticelli, with angelic features and a true, intrinsic and non-artificial beauty.

Two decades later, at their high school reunion in Ravenna, their paths converge again, but life has woven a different tapestry for each. Francesca finds herself ensnared by her father's debts, while David, once known as the shoemaker's son, now basks in the limelight of Milan's success with his own fashion business. Amidst the whirlwind of change, one thing remains unchanged – David's unwavering feelings for Francesca.

What David doesn't know is that Francesca's heart has never stopped beating for him. And never will.

Printed in Great Britain
by Amazon